Lionel Smith Beale

Life theories; their influence upon religious thought

Lionel Smith Beale

Life theories; their influence upon religious thought

ISBN/EAN: 9783337263997

Printed in Europe, USA, Canada, Australia, Japan

Cover: Foto ©Andreas Hilbeck / pixelio.de

More available books at **www.hansebooks.com**

LIFE THEORIES:

THEIR

INFLUENCE UPON RELIGIOUS THOUGHT.

"   — but if I could understand
" What you are, root and all, and all in all,
" I should know what God and man is."

LIFE THEORIES:

THEIR INFLUENCE

UPON

RELIGIOUS THOUGHT.

BY

LIONEL S. BEALE, M.B., F.R.S.,

Fellow of the Royal College of Physicians; Physician to King's College Hospital, and formerly Professor of Physiology and of General and Morbid Anatomy in King's College, London.

WITH SIX COLOURED PLATES.

LONDON :

HARRISON AND SONS, PRINTERS IN ORDINARY TO HER MAJESTY,
ST. MARTIN'S LANE.

PREFACE.

In this work I have adduced some of the reasons which have led me to think that the physical doctrine of life is opposed to the development of religious thought and natural theology, and adverse to scientific progress.

It has not been shown that any one of the physical or chemical hypotheses of life yet proposed rests upon the secure foundation of observation and experiment, while on the other hand the phenomena of living beings, open to the observation of all, not only justify the acceptance of a vital theory, but are only in this way to be accounted for.

Although it has been repeatedly affirmed that the *non-living* passes by insensible gradations into the *living*, no example of matter in the supposed transitional condition has yet been obtained, while, on the other hand, the facts which lead me to conclude that the difference between the living and the non-living is *absolute*, have neither been controverted nor explained away. My conclusions are indeed at variance with the views very generally entertained and taught in these days, but the truthfulness of the observations upon which they are based, now extending over a period of nearly twenty years, has not been called in question.

A portion of the first part of this essay has been printed in the *Contemporary Review* for April, 1871, but the argument has since been extended and further illustrated.

L. S. B.

61, *Grosvenor Street,*
    May, 1871.

TABLE OF CONTENTS.

I. Physical Life-theories and Religious Thought.

II. The Theory of Vitality and Religious Thought.

TABLE OF CONTENTS.

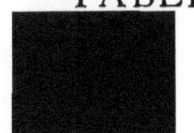

PLATES.

₊ The bioplasm, or living matter, which alone takes part in development and formation, is represented red in all these plates; the vessels blue, and the tissue, or formed material, in ordinary black ink.

PAGE

PART I.

PHYSICAL LIFE THEORIES

AND

RELIGIOUS THOUGHT.

PART II.

THE THEORY OF VITALITY

AND

RELIGIOUS THOUGHT.

"The existence of God, and the Immortality of the Soul, are not given us as phenomena, as objects of immediate knowledge ; yet, if the phenomena actually given do necessarily require, for their rational explanation, the hypothesis of Immortality and of God, we are assuredly entitled, from the existence of the former, to infer the reality of the latter."—Sir William Hamilton's Lectures—Lecture VII.

PHYSICAL LIFE THEORIES

RELIGIOUS THOUGHT.

F the progress of science is of necessity
associated with the decline of religious
belief, the hostility of religious persons to
science would be pardonable, if not reasonable and justifiable, for it has never been proved that
scientific information can, with advantage to the individual or to society, be substituted for religious teaching. Moreover, of a given number of persons, but a
small minority would be found capable of gaining real
proficiency in any branch of science, while it must be
admitted that almost everyone would make at least
considerable progress in religious knowledge. Although it is an open question whether the character is
necessarily or almost certainly improved by the study
of science, the influence of religious thought for good
in innumerable instances, and at every period of
history, will not be seriously disputed.

Religion and Science.—But is it true that religion
and science are hostile ? That reason and faith are

B

irreconcileable? That a man who has the gift of science must ever be wanting in the gift of faith? That the truths of religion are parted from the truths of science, and that he who devotes himself to scientific work, can take little interest in, and be little influenced by, religious thought?

Many, I fear, would answer these questions affirmatively. Some would go so far as to say that the tendencies of religious thought and the tendencies of scientific thought are in opposite directions, and that every attempt hitherto made to reconcile the teachings of science and religion has failed. Nevertheless I venture to think, and in this work I shall endeavour to give reasons for the conclusion, that the reply to all these questions should be made in the negative.

Authoritative Science.—Sufficient distinction has not, I think, been drawn by many who devote their lives mainly to religious thought and work, between science, and the statements put forward in her name—between scientific demonstration, and facts said to have been demonstrated by investigations called scientific—between the actual discovery of new truths proved beyond all question, and mere assertions sufficiently dogmatic, dictatorial, and positive, but resting upon authority instead of upon evidence.

Authoritative assertion damages the interests of science, and arrests the progress of truth, for science can never acknowledge any authority whatever. Her truths rest simply upon evidence, and the more carefully and the more minutely the evidence is sifted, the greater is the gain to science. Unfortunately, however, in every stage of scientific progress instances are not wanting in which mere positive assertions have been implicitly believed, and when these have been proved to be erroneous, new assertions as positive have taken their place, to be in their turn refuted and replaced by others. And this must ever be if people persist in accepting scientific statements upon authority alone, and refuse to study the grounds upon which the statements are said to rest.

Premature Concession.—A vague feeling of uncertainty has long prevailed in the minds of many highly educated persons with regard to the bearing of recently asserted scientific facts upon the beliefs which constitute the very foundations of religion. Rather than take the trouble even to ascertain the meaning of an assertion put forth, not a few accept it at once, and with it the state of mental perplexity which its acceptance involves. But surely it is most necessary that before a new doctrine or a new philosophy is violently opposed, because its influence on religious thought is likely to be prejudicial, or warmly accepted for the very same reason, or for a very different reason, it should be ascertained whether it rests upon demonstrated facts, or is a mere dictum, guess, or conjecture, of some authority.

I have sometimes suspected that some theologians in these days were prepared to concede too much, nay, to concede what will eventually prove to be the key of the position, regarded from the intellectual side. The proposition seems to have been accepted by many as proved, that the laws governing the living are the same as those which the *non-living* obey. But such a conclusion cannot reasonably be entertained at this time, nor is it likely that it will ever be proved to rest upon facts. The chivalrous generosity and large-heartedness of some minds, an intense love for everything that seems to favour progress, a desire to encourage investigation and work, and a natural hatred of narrow-mindedness and party prejudice, have perhaps led some thoughtful persons to accept for demonstrated facts, without the slightest investigation or inquiry, some of the most extraordinary statements ever promulgated in the name of truth, and to believe in all seriousness general propositions which, regarded from a scientific stand-point, are untenable ; as, for example, " the sun forms living beings," " the lifeless passes by gradations into the living," " the difference between a living thing and a dead one is a difference of degree," " a dead thing may be revivified," and many more quite as astounding. Such doctrines rest upon no scientific evidence whatever, and those who believe them receive them upon trust, and do not venture to inquire concerning the facts upon which they are said to rest.

Influence of Views on the Nature of Life upon Religious Thought.—Of all departments of scientific investigation, the one which concerns itself with the study of living beings is that which is calculated to exert the most serious influence upon religious thought, and it is especially to this I venture to direct attention in this book. It is, indeed, in connection with views concerning the nature of life that the most distinct antagonism between religion and science will be found to obtain.

Thoughtful men have allowed their judgment to be swayed by what seemed to them to be new discoveries of paramount importance, although they have not unfrequently experienced the greatest difficulty in grasping the meaning of the terms in which a discovery has been announced, and have not perhaps fully appreciated the consequences which must necessarily flow from the premisses they have accepted. For some years past there has been in England a powerful current setting in one direction, into which men have allowed themselves to be drawn, against the promptings of their feelings and sometimes against the dictates of their reason. They have been told, in language more forcible than convincing, that the facts of science demanded acquiescence, because the facts of science were incontrovertible, that truths established by observation and experiment were of all truths the most real, the most certain, and the most pure. But too frequently the assertions concerning certain so-called facts of science, after being carefully considered and examined, become resolved into the vaguest conjectures. Such, indeed, are many of the statements which have been made about the formative and constructive capacity of force. Energy does not construct or form, although it has been affirmed over and over again that it does *form* living things, that force *constructs* the worm and forms the bee, and that suns, the fountains of force, resolve themselves into the living beings that people this earth! But where is the evidence in favour of the constructive power of force? Is it not strange that anyone should maintain that force should be competent to construct the marvellous mechanism of a living plant or animal, when he must needs confess that all force is impotent to make a wheel or build a mill? But force is actually opposed to construction, and before anything can be built up, the tendencies of force must be overcome by *formative agency* or power. Unless force is first conquered, and then regulated and directed, structure will not be evolved. Force may destroy and dissipate, but it cannot build; it may disintegrate, but it cannot fashion; it may crush, but it is powerless to create. It is doubtful if it would be possible to adduce a dogma more unfounded than the dogma that the sun forms or builds—constructs or resolves itself into anything that possesses structure, and is capable of performing definite work of any kind for any purpose.

Men who have gained a scientific reputation in special departments have not hesitated to repudiate or condemn other branches of knowledge and other lines of inquiry, of the merits or advantages of which they are quite unable to form a correct estimate.

Physicists and chemists have disparaged microscopical inquiry, the remarks they have themselves made proving distinctly enough that they knew nothing of the question upon which they express most confident opinions. Of all departments of knowledge, the physiology of life has been the most unfortunate in this respect, and the most ridiculous statements about the nature of life have been approvingly sanctioned by men of high position in other branches of natural knowledge. Vitality has formed the favourite subject for perorations, and of late years many physical philosophers have concluded a long address, perhaps, on the nature and properties of the non-living, with some eloquent passages about the physical nature of life. Physicists have invaded a province of knowledge which they thought to conquer, but from which they must retire discomfited. They have laid down iron rules which they have been the first to disobey, and have protested loudly about the inexorable logic of facts, while they have themselves utterly discarded all fact—and, revelling in mere rhapsody and fancy, they have tried to convince the unlearned that they were teaching the facts of science. Physicists, without having studied the wonderful effects wrought by vitality, have tried hard to represent it as a slave of force, but it has proved, and will ever prove, its

master. Creative power is as far removed as ever
from non-constructing force ; and the great life-
mystery, in. spite of the efforts and consummate
skill of physicists and chemists, remains a mystery
as great as when in childhood the longing first arose
to inquire into the why and how.

If life is force, the idea of a Power higher than
force seems indeed superfluous. If life is but a form or
mode of ordinary force—if the phenomena of living
beings are the same in essential nature as the phenomena of lifeless matter—if the laws which govern
matter alive are the same as those which the non-
living and the dead must obey, all thought which
carries us beyond the experience of the organs of
our senses must be void, profitless, and waste.

For if by the investigation of matter and its properties a sufficient explanation of the phenomena of
life can be obtained, is it not clear that we shall not,
in order to explain the facts of life, call in the aid of
an hypothesis which involves the existence of power,
agency, force, or property altogether distinct from
the matter and the ordinary properties of material
particles ? But if, on the other hand, the phenomena
of living beings cannot be fully accounted for by
physics and chemistry, then it is a question still
open for discussion whether or not life is due to the
working of some agency or power distinct from
matter, and the idea of a much higher Power capable
of influencing all matter may not only be entertained

without inconsistency, but an additional argument is gained in its support.

Physical Theory of Life incompatible with Religious Thought.—If it were true that the facts of science really taught that all phenomena peculiar to living beings were in reality only physical and chemical phenomena, the very ground out of which all religious thought springs would be dissipated. For if I was sure that the formation of my body and the action of the living matter within me were certainly due to the properties of the particles of which my framework is constructed, how could I believe that I was, nevertheless, designed and created by the power and wisdom of God? If that were so, I should not seem to be nearer to the only sort of Deity admissible in such an order of things than the dust I tread upon, from which my body was made, and to which it will return; or than the wood and clay which may be so wonderfully fashioned by the hands and minds of men—nay, the latter would have for me far higher interest than any such Deity could possibly possess. For at best such a power could only affect me through matter, and could not be supposed to possess any sort of relation to me that a being capable of thinking and fashioning would care to acknowledge. I must believe that I was not related to my Maker in any way distinct or different from that in which the stone is related to its Maker. Nay, the stone and I would be particles, perhaps a little *modified*, in the same

order of things ; each occupying its place and performing its part in this world ; each dependent upon
the influences determined by conditions outside it,
each subject to be split up into its component molecules, to be scattered far and wide, perhaps to be
recombined at once into new forms, perhaps to be
distributed, and for ages, as cosmic mist.

Is Life a Consequence of Physical Actions only?—
Given the sun, gravitation, and all the secondary
mighty physical phenomena of nature, thunder, lightning, wind, rain, dew, and the like, did life follow as a
necessary consequence ? Might not the physical conditions of our planet as regards light, heat, and
moisture, have existed for ever without life having
been called forth ? The thunder may be God's voice,
but in living things, does not God speak in another
voice, and to man's spiritual nature with yet another ?
Why are we to accept the dictum of those who assert
that the laws which govern the non-living matter,
living matter, and the mind of man, are the same laws?
The two last have nothing in common with the first.
Where is the analogy between the inanimate stone
and the simplest living thing ? Does the stone, like
the living particle, convert matter of different composition into substances like those of which it consists,
and then divide and subdivide into little stones ?
Does it grow towards heaven like the tree, against the
laws of gravitation ?

The idea of a very remote or self-extinguished Crea-

tor.—Nor does it seem to me that I should be raised much higher than the stone among things created, if believing that, although I was really made by force, the workmanship of the sun, the constructing force of the sun which made me sprang direct from God. But if man has been formed by the sun, he at least is certain that he is endowed with powers higher than any the sun possesses, and is a being superior to the sun, in that he can form, and mould, and build, and fashion as he will. He knows that the sun is mere matter, and is not, like himself, endowed with reason, with power to discover the constitution of the distant suns, and tell the nature of the matter of which they are made. How therefore, knowing this, can man, being so much higher than the mere matter of the sun, submit to acknowledge it or its forces as his Creator?

And surely few can see much grandeur in the idea that the existing order of things here has resulted from an oscillation of an evolutional wave, which received its first impulse from the Infinite, into which its last undulations will merge. And few, one would think, can derive consolation, satisfaction, or hope from the idea of an All-powerful, who ceased to exert power ere this world was formed, and before the conditions resulting in the evolution of life were unconscious possibilities. Man would take little interest in so remote and indirect a Providence, and would rebel against the acknowledgment of a self-extinguished

Creator, or a God reposing powerless beyond the sun. If it were boldly affirmed that in these latter days the God of the beginning, the great First Cause, had ceased to be, it is doubtful if man *could* force himself to believe that any lifeless forces or elements were endowed with designing or creative power, for is it possible to conceive of such transcendent powers, except as attributes of an ever-living, ever-acting Infinite?

Of Power and Force.—I beg the reader to consider the vast difference between power, force, and property, for these are quite distinct from one another. Power is capable of activity; it may design, arrange, form, construct, build. Property is passive, and belongs to the material particles, and is no more capable of destruction than the particles themselves. Force differs from property, in that its form or mode may be changed or conditioned and assume other forms, and be afterwards restored to the original one.

Power may cease and vanish, but property is retained, and force in one form or other is persistent. Neither matter, nor force, nor property, can wholly disappear; but all order, design, arrangement, guidance, form, structure, construction, may vanish. Power alone imposes upon the material the wonderful order which everywhere manifests itself in nature. The property of the material renders such imposition possible, but does not effect it. Were the particles of our planet distributed in a manner ever so chaotic and meaningless, matter and force might be, grain for grain, foot-pound for foot-pound, property for property, as in the existing order of things. Nor could the mighty differences between the supposed and the present condition be expressed in force or property terms.

But let me not offend those who differ from me by mere words. I care not whether the term *power* be accepted or discarded in favour of some other word. The name given to the designing, arranging, and governing capacity is a matter of absolute indifference to me. But I cannot allow, without a protest, that the faculty itself should be ignored, and people told that all the phenomena manifested in the material world are to be accounted for by the properties and forces of the material molecules themselves, for that is a dogma which cannot be tenable—a mere dictum of pretentious self-asserting authority, misleading, confusing, untrustworthy.

Self-constructing Properties of Molecules.—The idea that the form and structure of living beings are to be attributed to the properties of the particles of matter of which they are made, and the influences to which these particles are exposed when they come together, is, however, at this very time, nevertheless, seriously entertained and taught. It has indeed been definitely stated, and the statement has been repeated more than once, that the whole "world, living and non-living," has resulted by the "mutual interaction" of the "forces possessed by the molecules of which the primitive nebulosity of the universe was composed."

The sentence following this nebulous assertion shows in what impenetrable mists Mr. Huxley has lost himself. If the above view about primitive nebulosity be true, he goes on to say, "it is no less certain that the existing world lay, potentially, in the cosmic vapour; and that a sufficient intelligence could, from a knowledge of the properties of the molecules of that vapour, have predicted, say the state of the Fauna of Britain in 1869, with *as much certainty* as one can say what will happen to the vapour of the breath in a cold winter's day." But who cares to learn what a supposititious intelligence, having knowledge unknowable, might have predicted concerning the hypothetical molecules of an apocryphal primeval mist, under circumstances which, had they existed, would have rendered impossible the existence of the intelligence?

The idea incompatible with the ideas of Providence, Personal God, and Christianity.—If the formation and action of our tissues and organs are really due to the properties of the particles constituting the materials of our body, it is difficult to understand what influence a God could be supposed to exert after the particles had been created in the first beginning, and had been endowed with their properties. Does not such doctrine, I would ask, strike at the root of the idea of a living God, and aim at accounting for all the phenomena of this world by law, independent of will, power, or design? In such a scheme neither a Superintending Providence, nor a Personal God, nor Christianity could have place. It remains only to ask whether the mind can be satisfied to regard Deity merely as a primeval creative impulse, of which everything that has since happened and will happen is a consequence; and to inquire further, whether it would be possible for us to draw any distinction between a relationship to a first cause, so very inappreciable, indirect, and remote, and an absence of any relationship whatever.

Failure of Attempts to Construct Living Beings.— According to many, for years past we seem to have been on the eve of discovering the conditions under which the component elements of the organisms of living beings could be made to combine to form the organic compounds, and these compounds made to live. It has indeed been affirmed, over and over again, that the morning of discovery has dawned, nay, that the living has been actually formed direct from the non-living; but the spontaneous ovum has yet to be exhibited,—the living jelly has yet to be evolved from the laboratory-bred plasma.

Failure of Analogical Reasoning, Metaphor, and Prophecy.—Notwithstanding the most ingenious attempts and long-sustained efforts, it has been found impossible to make any form of apparatus, or to obtain any chemical substance which acts like a living body, or which could possibly be mistaken for matter that was alive. Attempts have therefore been made to prove that between certain non-living things and living things there existed some analogy. And while it has been reluctantly admitted, in a vague sort of way, that there *is* a difference between the living and the non-living, the analogies which had already been demonstrated, justified, it was said, the anticipation that, as science was continually advancing, a time would come when means would be discovered by which the non-living should be made to exhibit the phenomena which are now regarded by some of us as peculiar to the living world.

As all efforts to make living things failed, it was only natural that those sanguine persons, who had determined that success shall be attained some day, should endeavour to keep hope alive by resorting to metaphor, and calling in the aid of analogical reasoning. But the argument from analogy has been tremendously strained. Life, which arranges and gives to matter form and structure, has been likened to flame, which involves the disintegration of matter, and which destroys all form and structure. The living thing, it has been said, is like the crystal, as if the living thing was at its formation deposited from a solution, and could be dissolved and re-crystallised as often as we will.

Man has been represented as something between a crystal, which may, by mere change in temperature, be precipitated from, and then dissolved again in, its own mother-liquor, and a clock, that ticks away its existence till its works are worn out or are choked by dust, or ceases more suddenly from its time-marking labours, in consequence of the breaking of the spring, or the falling of its weights, when its works are thrown into the melting pot, and there is an end of that particular clock.

A living creature, it has been affirmed, is analogous to a machine, which goes when it is wound up, or when water is placed in its boiler and fire in its grate, as if the fire could be re-lighted after it had once gone out, and a *living machine* be made to go again after it had once stopped. But there is not even an analogy between a machine and a living thing in construction. For is not each portion of the machine first made and finished, and then fitted carefully to others, when the machine becomes complete, and is at last ready for work? But work construction of the living machine is carried out in a very different way, and upon very different principles. All the several parts are connected from the very first. Each portion is developed in its proper place, and requires no fitting or adaptation whatever. Every part is evolved out of the structureless, or rather seems to evolve itself. Neither tools nor any kind of mechanism are concerned in its production.

It has been shown that from all living things an albuminous substance may be obtained. Therefore, it has been affirmed, living matter is albuminous—as if there was no difference between living matter and the albuminous substances which result after the matter has ceased to live. Still it was found necessary in some instances to admit that a guiding or directing influence of some kind did exist. As it had been shown that force could not guide matter, the difficulty was solved by affirming that matter guided the force. But of course no explanation of what was meant by the phrase "guiding physical forces," was offered, and if anyone inquired he would probably have been told that his question was frivolous.

Some philosophers, distinguished for their zeal to establish the physical doctrine of life, have imagined that they possessed the gift of prophecy. Though fact and law and logic had their advantages, proof of their view, which was not attainable now, would certainly be forthcoming at some not very distant period of time. Everything tended towards a physical explanation of vital phenomena, and it was affirmed that the tendency would continue. But prophecies and tendencies have never exerted much influence upon scientific discovery. The scientific man who prophecies, forsakes the straight path into which he has been led by observation and experiment, and thereby acknowledges his mistrust in the scientific principles in which he professed to believe, if indeed he does not take the path which leads towards the doctrine of infallibility, so fatal to the law of progress.

If the Physical Doctrine of Life is accepted, must not the idea of God be given up ?—If the physical view be accepted, surely the abandonment of the idea of a God, of Divinity of every kind, of immortality, and free agency, is only a question of time. And yet it seems scarcely credible that any one could have seriously concluded that ere long physics would replace the old beliefs, and that, although comparatively few of us were yet sufficiently intelligent or were too bigoted to renounce the simple faith imbibed in our childhood, as our knowledge increased our prejudices would wane, and we should at last discard religion altogether, and accept as a substitute for it faith in the omnipotence of force.

But are not such ideas as Omniscience, Omnipotence, design and power, as far removed from physical philosophy, with its immutable laws and necessary sequences, as is the idea of a personal God?

If the formation of a living organism had been an exceptional or only a very occasional phenomenon, is it not exceedingly probable that it would have been regarded as miraculous? The frequency of its occurrence, and our familiarity with the fact of the continual formation of living things, alone prevent the operation from being attributed to preternatural agency. Regarded from a merely physico-chemical, or, as some would say, scientific stand-point, the production of every living thing is indeed preternatural, inasmuch as the process cannot be explained by any laws of nature yet discovered. The physical philosopher may triumphantly exclaim, " fact I know, and law I know." But his philosophy does not yet enable him to explain how lifeless matter comes to live, so he cuts the knot by declaring that force is, and that life other than force cannot be.

Advocates of Physical View of Life not active Opponents of Religion.—It cannot be maintained that those who support the physical theory of life have taken any active part in opposing religion, nor have physical and chemical doctrines been advanced as antagonistic to religious thought. It would appear rather as if the advocates of these views only desired that they should be taught far and wide, and that it should be left to the people instructed to discover whether the enlightened doctrine was consistent or not with their religious prejudices. Still, it must, I think, be obvious to thoughtful persons, that the view that man is a mere machine, constructed by force, whose structure and actions depend upon the properties of the material particles of which his body is composed, and the influence of physical agencies upon these, is scarcely reconcileable with the idea that man is made in the image of God, and that man holds or can ever hold communion with his Maker.

But theories in high favour in these days, and very widely taught, rest upon the assumption that an interval of-time, so great as to be reckoned by ages, and far beyond computation, separates the existing living creation from its Creator. God is removed farther and farther from us, until the conception is utterly lost in the dim twilight of the infinitely remote beginning, and man is left alone, by unintelligent conditions, in a wilderness of unconscious molecules, himself the victim of laws which his atoms are forced to obey, while he is unconscious of the terms imposed, and utterly unable to find them out. Man, the only creature able to invent and design, is no more than one of an infinite number of expressions of the stuff he feeds upon, a mere transient image, of far less importance than the active everlasting indestructible atoms of his body, which have directly emanated from the infinitely remote and self-extinguished first cause, the origin and source of all.

If modern Theories true, a revolution in Religious Belief must occur.—But it is certain that if the doctrines which have been lately so strongly advocated had been proved to rest upon a sure foundation, a complete and wide-spread revolution in religious belief would have occurred. If the discovery of the way in which the non-living can be directly converted into the living, should at any time be made, a mighty change in thought will indeed be inaugurated. A change in philosophy, greater than has ever taken place, would in that case commence, nor would it cease to progress until every old world view had given place to new ideas. Such a discovery would be regarded, and, I venture to think, rightly regarded, as a new revelation.

If a particle of living matter, not more than $\frac{1}{100000}$th of an inch in diameter, were made in the laboratory out of non-living matter—if it lived and moved, and grew and multiplied, I confess my belief in "the spiritual nature of my faculties" would be severely shaken. Many, whose opinion is entitled to the greatest respect, would, I know, be inclined to answer, that a man who rested all on such an accident of scientific discovery as this, could have no faith. But would anyone who had formed a true conception of the nature and attributes of a living particle, believe that there is the slightest probability of such a particle ever being manufactured? Each step in investigation seems to separate such a theoretical possibility farther and farther from the real and actual. Of course it will be remarked, " it is nevertheless possible that a living particle *may* be made some day." But can it be proved to be impossible that a whale or an elephant should be constructed out of the non-living at some future time?

Most recent conjectures and fancies concerning the Nature and Origin of Living Beings.—Quite recently speculations concerning the mechanical nature of vital actions have been supplemented by vague conjectures about the *universal* distribution of *spirit*, and the union between spirit and matter. The matter may be so very attenuated and minutely divided, that it is quite impossible to conceive further attenuation and division, without losing altogether the conception of matter. For it would appear that many cubic leagues of the matter united with its spirit would not turn the scale of the most delicate balance.

Whether the "spirit" of 1870 is some new mode of force capable of assuming the form of *heat* or *motion*, or modified force of another kind, or an agency altogether distinct from any force yet discovered—an actual, tangible spirit, evolved in the course of new observations and experiments not yet communicated to us, or a mere fiction emanating from the fancy of a privileged spirit, has yet to be ascertained. The spirit in question has, however, been associated with matter, at an immense height above the earth, and for a very long period of time,—with the matter constituting the blue sky, which, like the undifferentiated primeval mist out of which worlds are formed, is, we are told, redolent of life. How the fact has been ascertained is not stated, but every statement advanced by the physicist rests upon the inexorable logic of facts, so perhaps facts are forthcoming. It would, however, be interesting to have the evidence in detail which proves that life is abundant in the blue sky, for even the "eye of intellect" is scarcely "hard and sharp" enough to see the latent life amongst such misty attenuated spirit-matter. Nor can it be supposed that by the most ingenious mechanical contrivance which the physicist could devise, could we succeed in obtaining even the smallest trace of blue sky for physical or chemical examination in the laboratory. Only the wildest fancy would suggest for an instant that what is termed *life* could exist up there. The latent life of the blue sky must at any rate be very latent indeed, and it must be a different *mode* of life from the mortal form met with here. But these questions will perhaps be considered when further inquiries into the nature of blue sky-matter have been made and the results communicated.

Although the sky-matter is in such a very minute state of division that the whole belonging to our globe might be packed in a snuff-box, all the *philosophy, poetry, science, and art of a future age* must, it is confidently affirmed, be latent in it. Whether the spirit of the blue sky matter is a different mode or form of the same spirit that is at work in the living matter of the surface of the earth, or a different kind of spirit altogether, seems to be still open to discussion.

It is somewhat difficult for any ordinary working living spirit to track his way through the attenuated mist-science which has been recently evolved from the physical imaginations of privileged spirits. And it is doubtful if much will be gained on the part of the mere observer, fact-hunter, or experimenter by the most careful examination of " the idea of primeval union between spirit and matter," since its author seems to have experienced so much difficulty in making his meaning clear, that he has been obliged to make use of an extract from the marriage service to illustrate his view of the mode of union which prevails, and to attest his indignation at the idea of the possibility of the connection between spirit and matter ever being severed by a power so feeble as that of man.

With reference to living matter, physicists do permit us to teach that this is structureless, and even Dr. Tyndall would probably for the present tolerate the view that no machinery, either molecular or of any other kind, which would enable him to account for the phenomena invariably manifested by living matter, can be discovered by the microscope. But such a difficulty is only apparent. It cannot, says the lecturer, " be too distinctly borne in mind that between the microscope limit and the *true (!)* molecular limit there is room for infinite permutations and combinations." But, unfortunately, he knows nothing about the *microscope limit*, nor the *true molecular limit*, nor the *room* between the two, nor the *permutations*, nor the *combinations*. Here, then, is an excellent example of the physical-fact logic of one who has long maintained that physics will account for vital phenomena. But, strange as it may appear, this authority is at last forced to admit that he has called in the aid of his imagination, and some of his pupils may be led to teach that there is more science to be learnt in the realms of fancy and in dream-land than by observation and experiment. The attempt to restrict the use of the imagination to " privileged spirits " only, does not indicate a generous or philosophical disposition.

Dr. Tyndall's argument against the microscope may be put thus. It is certain that many facts remain undiscovered beyond the microscope limit, and if these apocryphal facts were discovered they might justify conclusions different from those already deduced from the facts of observation. In other words, facts which can be demonstrated are of little value or importance, because *beyond* the limits of investigation may be some unascertained facts which, if they could be discovered, might be found to outweigh the actual facts.

It so happens that certain facts already demonstrated by the microscope, but which Dr. Tyndall will not acknowledge, are more than sufficient to controvert the hypothesis he has unfortunately so widely and so energetically taught. These facts of microscope observation and investigation are well known to many observers, and the bearing of them has been explained in language which, though less forcible, is perhaps not less intelligible than that in which the fancy facts of the imagination have been introduced to the public.

There are surely few scientific facts likely to be of greater value in the education of young people of both sexes than those elucidated by the aid of the microscope, but it unfortunately happens that the general conclusions which the pupil would arrive at from microscope studies would be likely to lead him to reject the physical hypotheses of life, and to convince him that these were incompetent to explain the facts of observation.

In the region beyond the microscope limit, says Dr. Tyndall, "the poles of the atoms are arranged, that tendency is given to their powers, so that when the poles and powers have free action, and proper stimulus in a suitable environment, they determine first the germ, and afterwards the complete organism." My physical knowledge is not sufficient to enable me to understand this, but it may be calculated to convey much real information to the people. Perhaps it is not surprising that one who holds such views should believe, and endeavour to make others accept the doctrine, that "the human mind itself— emotion, intellect, will, and all their phenomena— were once latent in a fiery cloud." "Many who hold the hypothesis of natural evolution," says Dr. Tyndall, "would probably assent to the position that at the present moment all our philosophy, all our poetry, all our science, all our art—Plato, Shakespeare, Newton, and Da Vinci—are potential in the fires of the sun." But probably a long course of training would be insufficient to enable any one to assent to this position, unless he had had the advantage of being born a privileged spirit.

It is very well for authority to exclaim, "Let us reduce, *if we can (!)*, the visible phenomena of life to mechanical attractions and repulsions," let us cast "the term 'vital force' from our vocabulary,"

and so on ; but though he and others have the will to
do all this, and full confidence in their prospects of
success, the attempt has been so far a failure. Life
cannot be reduced to mechanical attractions and repulsions, nor can any attractions and repulsions be
made to imitate the phenomena of life. Dr. Tyndall
may cast any word he pleases from his vocabulary,
but it may nevertheless remain in the world's vocabulary as long as the thing which it signifies continues to exist.

No doubt many scientific men desire above all
things that people should believe that life is only
physical change, but as they cannot bring forward
evidence to convince the reason, they seem to be
trying hard to gain assent by the aid of strong
assertions, by a little gently expressed contempt for
other views, and occasionally by a dexterous effort
violently to overwhelm, or silence, or extinguish their
opponents by force. The most conspicuous member
of this class of "privileged spirits" speaks of a student
of natural knowledge as a "microscopist, ignorant
alike of philosophy and biology," and belonging to
a college "famous for orthodoxy."* It is desirable
to examine very carefully the dogmatic assertions of
spirits who consider themselves privileged to employ
this mode of gaining converts, and enforcing their own
principles.

* " Essays on the Use and Limit of the Imagination in Science,"
second edition, page 49.

What has been gained by the Physical Hypothesis of Life?—For many years past the advocates of various physical doctrines of life have been encouraged in every possible way. A large section of the public, it appears, has desired to be taught such views. The statements have been heartily welcomed by the most advanced writers in the periodical literature of our time, who have hailed vague assertions as brilliant discoveries. The merest shadow which appeared to tell in favour of a material hypothesis has been repeated, embellished, and forced into notoriety; while researches, in the course of which facts have been discovered which seemed favourable to other hypotheses, have been rejected with contempt, or ignored. The supporters of physical doctrines of life have assisted one another, fought for one another, and praised one another. They have exhibited such determination, and have employed such strong language, as to intimidate many of those who differ from them. Consequently their views have been but little questioned, and, for the most part, instead of being subjected to searching criticism, have been praised, and in no doubtful terms. Physicists have of late been high in popular favour, and have in fact enjoyed every advantage which the most zealous partisans of a cause could desire. But what have they effected? What solid advantage has the public gained by their teaching, carried on in the most zealous manner for twenty years? Have they suc-

ceeded in establishing their principles, or are they
likely to succeed in doing so within any reasonable
period of time? Are their conclusions accepted,
or their arguments respected by careful thoughtful
persons?

I have already endeavoured to reply to some of
these questions, but a few words as to the results produced by physical hypotheses may not be out of place
here. I need only refer to some observations in a
leading article in the leading journal of this country (?)
for September 19th, 1870. These will enable us
to form some idea of the effects of twenty years'
active advocacy of such hypotheses upon the minds
even of highly intelligent persons. The " Times "
tells the British public that the researches of *natural
philosophers* seem to show that all the world, or at
least all living things, are nothing but large boxes
containing *an infinite number of little boxes one within
the other, and that the least and tiniest box of all contains the " germ!"* Now, if for germ we substitute
" intelligence," and look upon each of the boxes as
a new layer of conjecture, successively applied to im-
prison more and more securely the understanding,
already effectually shut up in box number one, we shall
get a not inapt illustration of the influence the new
philosophy has had upon the mind of the writer of the
article, and possibly also upon the minds of many willing and enthralled disciples. Perhaps the writer was
the same enthusiast whose words have been quoted

by Dr. Tyndall under the head of " Pros and Cons." "We saw in imagination the victory of conscience and reason, the emancipation of a soul, the new birth of an intelligence," and so on.*

Those who attentively study the expositions of the physical school, will find that, instead of facts, hypothesis has been piled upon hypothesis, and assertion heaped upon assertion, the whole resting upon a basis of continually shifting assumption. Not even the words and phrases used in enunciating the physical doctrines of vitality are permitted to retain precisely the same meaning throughout one single communication. Confusion succeeds confusion. There is, however, that one idea—that the living and the non-living are one, and are influenced by physical forces only— which ever brightly shines through the mists of the modern nebulous philosophy, and illumines its attendant satellites. This all obey, and around it all revolve.

No physical theory of Life yet propounded stands the test of careful examination.—In my work on " Protoplasm, or Matter, Life, and Mind," published some months since, I have examined several physical theories of life which have received many advocates, and have

---

* But alas, *tempora mutantur!* Ere seven months have gone, another writer in the " Times " sees fit to complain of the " unscientific enthusiasm " with which Dr. Tyndall had dilated on the use of the imagination in science, and with stern disapprobation ousts the autumnal hymn of praise.

been most warmly supported during the last twenty years. Not one of them, however, is found to stand the test of careful critical analysis. Each breaks down, and completely, upon examination, and the last proposed, and perhaps the most pretentious, is the weakest of them all. Many are so obviously inconsistent with facts known to almost everyone, that it is wonderful such notions should have been seriously advanced. After reviewing these hypotheses, the critic will be astonished that so many doctrines should have been put forward in so short a time in support of the physical view of life. He is almost forced to conclude that their authors must have had some strong motive for endeavouring to make people believe that a physical hypothesis in some shape or other must be received, and that no other explanation was possible. In their remarks upon vital physics, there is a total absence of that philosophical indifference which distinguishes the same writers when discussing some other matters. As soon as they enter upon the vital question, they assume the tone of the advocate, of the proselytizer, of the zealot, and to such energy everything must yield. They put before the reader only the arguments which seem to tell in favour of the doctrine they teach, and the importance of these is usually much exaggerated. The view must needs be supported by forced similes, overstrained analogies, and metaphors calculated to absorb the attention of the reader, and to interfere with his impartial consideration of the question. Not unfrequently the physical advocate excites the flagging interest of his pupils by an affirmation, a protest, a prophecy, or a declaration of his individual infallible conviction and belief. Unproven and unprovable assertions have been advanced over and over again, until it becomes tiresome to notice them.* The fallacy of the crystal argument has been many times exposed during the last hundred years, but there it stands in all its fictitious strength, in the very last work written in favour of the hapless spontaneous generation doctrine. Writers on the physical force side not unfrequently speak with contempt of the views of their opponents, while it is utterly impossible to get them to acknowledge that their own assertions should be subjected to any examination whatever, because, according to them, the physical view only is to be received. Some physical authorities are impatient of criticism, avoid debate, announce their views in sermons, and seem to be unable to distinguish between preaching and teaching. Objections which they cannot answer they affect to despise ; and, instead of mentioning the terms of the particular objections to which they refer, account opposition

---

* The sun " prepares the food which supplies our frames with energy as well as with that delicate tissue which is essential to our existence," is an example of the way physicists commonly state the case. They then go on to remark that the sun is a fire, forgetting how incorrect it would be to talk of a fire " preparing " our dinners or the latter supplying us with nerve and muscle and bone. Physicists should really study the structure and mode of growth of tissues before they talk of their preparation by the sun or speak of the great luminary as a creator.

D

" frivolous." Their plan of treating those who differ from them is like that of the boy who throws a stone or two, and then runs away.

But if any form of the physical doctrine of life had been proved to be true, or had been shown to be based upon some sort of trustworthy evidence, or had upon careful examination even appeared plausible, it would undoubtedly have been right to have inquired very carefully whether religious views could any longer be considered defencible. No one will deny that belief in any of the fanciful hypotheses of the last ten years is consistent with the display of virtues, called " Christian," though many are doubtful whether the physical doctrine is not inconsistent with a belief in the evidences of Christianity. But it has certainly to be shown that the evidence adduced in favour of physical views of life is strong enough to disturb, ever so slightly, the old foundations of Christian faith.

If many of the modern hypotheses concerning the nature of life were true, or even tended towards truth, it must be admitted their influence would be detrimental to religious thought. Indeed religious thought in the sense in which the term has been generally understood would probably soon be of the past.

The advocates of some of these doctrines appear to consider that the fancies they propound are to take the place of religious beliefs, and to supplant them, and are to form the basis of some new religion of the future. But it is not only as regards views concerning the nature of life that modern science aims at taking a very exalted place in human hopes and aspirations, for does not she claim to be able to solve with precision problems the solution of which no form of religion has hitherto ventured to do more than suggest, as it were, vaguely, diffidently, and doubtfully? Such, for example, as the mode of origin and formation of the world, the causes of the early changes upon its surface, the origin and nature of all living things, the precise relation of man to other beings, the end of all.

Every form of physical hypothesis involves the conviction on the part of its advocate that the evidence we possess justifies the belief that the present phenomena of existence are but a consequence of antecedent physical changes, these of others, and so on, as it were, in a chain, link succeeding link, up to the very first, which originated in the beginning. But the evidence hitherto advanced in favour of such a view is most inconclusive.

But is it not a fact of profound significance, that nothing whatever has been proved concerning the physical nature of the changes which immediately precede the production of a particle of secretion or of tissue in any living organism whatever? The changes are said to be molecular, but, what is molecular? and what precedes the occurrence of the supposed molecular change? Those who pretend to be able to tell us all about our origin from a fiery cloud in a remote past, are unable to inform us of the nature of the changes occurring in any part of one of the multitudes of living beings around us, and which changes are now proceeding from moment to moment under our very eyes. They tell us nothing of what takes place in the matter we can study and investigate, and expect us to receive without question the extravagant assertions they make concerning the changes which occurred in the primeval mist out of which our planet, with everything upon it, has, according to their statement, been formed. Not only so, but they do their best to suppress all theorizing and speculation concerning present life which does not happen to chime in with their dismal fancies concerning the past and future changes of their material molecules, and their melancholy views about evolution by what they call *law*, without any kind of superintending, or willing or designing, directing or governing power.

THE THEORY OF VITALITY

AND

RELIGIOUS THOUGHT.

———

I'T has been shown that the acceptance of any of the physical theories of life hitherto proposed, would involve the necessity of very serious alterations in our views concerning religion, and that if the physical doctrine of vitality could be proved to rest upon any basis of truth, the old foundations of religious thought, which were not completely destroyed, would have to be entirely reconstructed.

We have now to consider whether the theory of vitality to which one is led by a careful study of the changes occurring during the development and growth of every kind of living being known, will in any way affect the religious beliefs which have been entertained for many centuries by the best and wisest among men.

In the first place, it is necessary to state the theory and the grounds on which it rests. The doctrine of vitality, which the results of careful observation have led me to accept, involves the conclusion that living matter of every kind and description, and at every

period of life, is altogether different in its essential
nature from any kind of non-living matter whatever,
even so very different that there is a total absence of
any analogy between the properties peculiar to the
living matter and any properties known in connection
with the non-living. The transcendent difference is
not due to chemical composition or to physical constitution or property, but to the presence and activity
of a power which cannot, under any circumstances, be
developed from matter that has not been made to
live by the influence of that which is already living.

My investigations have been conducted in the hope
that, from a careful study of the character of the
acts performed, I might succeed in drawing an inference concerning the nature of the unknown power
that effects the wonderful changes which are inexplicable by any known laws, and cannot be accounted
for by any material agencies, properties, or forces.

*Phenomena of Living Matter different from Pheno-
mena of all Non-living Matter.*—Notwithstanding all
that has been *asserted*, over and over again, to the contrary, it has been proved conclusively that the phenomena of the simplest living thing are essentially
different from those of non-living matter, and cannot
be imitated, and that the living does not emanate
from the non-living, or pass into it by gradations.
Life is no mere sum of ordinary forces, nor does vital
action result from material changes alone. It cannot
be shown that the matter of the world and its mate-

rial forces necessarily give rise to the development of life. We may, therefore, still regard *life* as transcending mere matter and its forces—a later gift of an All-Wise Omnipotence.

The tiniest speck of living matter exhibits no structure to account for its actions, and it contains no machinery. It belongs to a system altogether different from the mechanical world. It is not in the least degree like a clock, for no two of its 'ticks' are alike. Every one of its molecules makes its own wheels and cranks and springs and pendulum, and sets itself going and winds itself up, and makes new clocks, and in a moment, as perfect and as powerful and as strong as the parent, and all this though completely destitute of *works* or *machinery* of any kind. And there are millions of such molecules in the most minute parts of every living organism. Many of them acting in harmony, now tending one way, now another; now appearing to obey gravitation, now moving, and with equal velocity, in defiance of the great law. To compare a living thing with a clock is, then, misleading, and it is perversely misleading. The molecules of matter that is alive are arranged as they were never before arranged. Elements which have the strongest affinity for one another are separated from their combinations, and perhaps made to combine with elements with which they have no natural tendency to unite; and all this is effected, not as we see it done in the laboratory by the skilful chemist after prolonged experience and with the aid of complex contrivances, but silently, and, as it were, by a *fiat*, without any apparatus whatever.

Of the Two States of Matter in Living Beings.—Some years ago, I obtained evidence which convinced me that the substance of the bodies of all things living was composed of matter in two states ; and I showed that the truly vital phonomena, *nutrition, growth, and multiplication*, were manifested by one of the two kinds of matter, while the other was the seat of physical and chemical changes only. From observations I was led to conclude, that of any living thing, but a part of the matter of which it was constituted, was really *living* at any moment. In the case of adult forms of the higher animals and man, indeed only a very small portion of the total quantity of their body-matter is alive at any period of existence.

These views met with little favour at the time, but have since been accepted by many. The facts upon which my arguments were based have not been disturbed by those who are opposed to my views. It has been asserted by some that the distinction between the living and non-living matter of a living being could not be sustained, and by others that such a distinction was of no importance at all, if it could be established.

Certain authorities have most positively affirmed that the living differs from the non-living only in degree, and that the non-living passes by gradations into the living, but they appeal to the imagination for the facts upon which their assertion is founded. Between the living and the non-living they say there is no essential difference—no difference save in the rate at which the physical and chemical changes are carried on. Any one might as well attempt to prove that the living state and the dead state were different degrees of one and the same state. But the living is not the lifeless, and it has been shown that matter in the former condition may be positively distinguished from matter in the latter state, even in the case of extremely minute particles in which living matter and matter that has ceased to live, and matter that is about to live, are associated together within a very small area.

Bioplasm or Living Matter.—It must be carefully borne in mind, that the *living matter* or *bioplasm* in which wonderful changes occur as long as its life lasts (which changes cannot be explained by physics and chemistry), is not a substance very sparingly distributed, and only occasionally to be separated from the living beings and studied, but it is to be found almost everywhere. It can be examined at any time, and the principal and most remarkable phenomena can be demonstrated with the aid of a $\frac{1}{12}$th of an inch object-glass magnifying 700 diameters. There is not a living being which does not contain *bioplasm*, and whose structure, composition, and actions do not depend upon it. There is not at any period of life, in health or in disease, a portion of any tissue of man's body the size of a pin's head, with perhaps the single exception of the teeth of the adult and in old age, that does not contain some of this living matter or *bioplasm* in which *purely vital phenomena* take place. Nor is there an action characteristic of living beings, at any period of their existence, in which this bioplasm does not play an all-important part. The germ at the earliest period is composed of it almost entirely, and from the original bioplasmic germ-mass results the infinite number of bioplasts which subsequently take part in the formation of the several tissues and organs.

Every tissue may be divided anatomically into *elementary parts.* Each elementary part consists of the *living matter* or *bioplasm,* and the *lifeless formed matter* (cell-wall, envelope, tissue, intercellular substance, periplastic matter) produced at the moment of the death of the particles of the first. *Formed matter* accumulates in the tissues as age advances, and thus interferes with the free access of nutrient matter to the bioplasm.

As we grow old the proportion of the living to the lifeless matter of the organism becomes less and less, but even in advanced age and in the driest of growing tissues, living matter is still to be demonstrated in considerable amount, and can be discovered in advanced age without difficulty.

That I may render the facts upon which my conclusions have been founded clear to the reader, I will

Fig. 1.

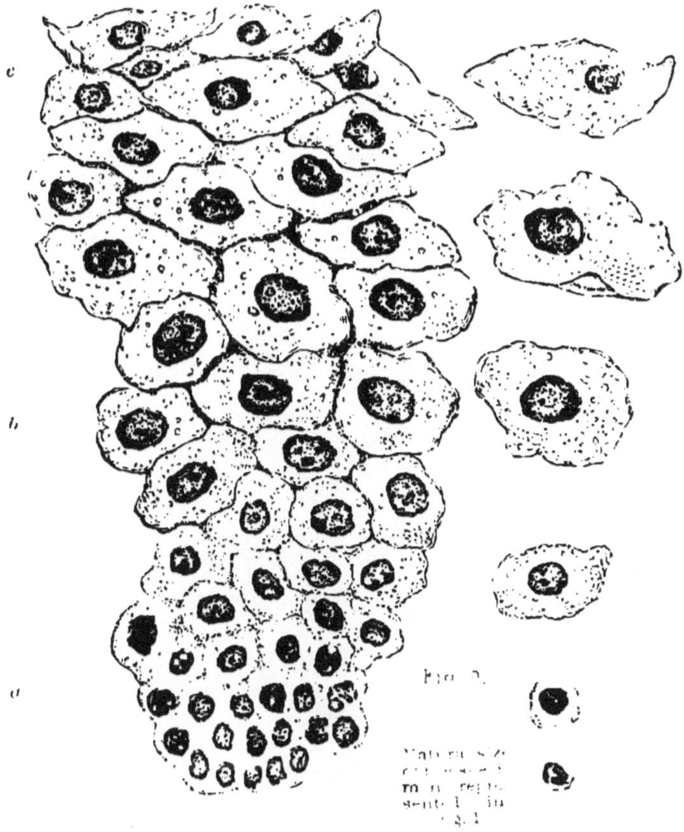

Fig. 2.

Perpendicular s . t.   h thick la   .   . fth t
the ti plasm a   att ca t the   th   t   t
part f the f ure, the c   s wh h ne   sed to   t all
SEPARA   str but the s b form lma   alt rns   s
ti plasts and a   m d plyin   When t   t an l n c   l as
be asın to sem x ut the p o css t mult   atic ens s   1   s al
the surface c to   e the pl ac   o l, s   mog c tl to u l n a   t
th remains of the biop lasm ma   c di   a tili 17   at t

$\frac{1}{1000}$ u 11 c   ʌ

ask him to examine attentively the drawings taken from a few very minute pieces of tissue which have been prepared so as to distinctly show the masses of bioplasm embedded in them, from which they were formed, and by the influence of which their integrity was preserved as long as life lasted.* Every mass of bioplasm of any tissue can be artificially and permanently coloured by an ammoniacal solution of carmine, and thus every particle of living matter in a tissue can be demonstrated very distinctly, and its relative proportion in the same tissue at different ages, accurately determined.† In the following drawings, copied from actual specimens, the bioplasm is coloured carmine red, the vessels which were injected with Prussian-blue fluid‡, blue, and the tissue or formed material is represented by the ordinary printing ink, because it was not coloured in the preparations.

Now, let us picture to ourselves in every part of the tissues of a living thing, even in the solid bone, Pl. II, fig. 1, and separated from one another by tolerably equal distances, little particles of living matter, often

---

* Many specimens, prepared in this manner, were demonstrated publicly in the Courses of Lectures given by me at the Royal College of Physicians in 1861, in King's College from 1858 to 1869, and in Oxford, by direction of the Radcliffe Trustees, in 1868–69. For details of the mode of preparation, *see* "How to Work with the Microscope," 4th edit., p. 108.

† If Mr. Huxley had studied specimens prepared in this manner, his views concerning Protoplasm would probably have been modified in very important particulars.

‡ "How to Work with the Microscope," pp. 93, 97.

less than the $\frac{1}{2000}$th of an inch in diameter, each
separated from its neighbours, and surrounded by
the material it has produced. Each living bioplast
attracting, through the lifeless matter already formed
by it, materials suitable for its nutrition. Each, living,
growing, and forming ; each capable of infinite
growth, infinite multiplication.

Bioplasm of Cuticular Covering of Tongue.—In the
first place let us study a minute particle of the tissue
which forms the upper free surface of the tongue, in
size much less than the head of a very small pin,
Plate I, fig. 2.   When this is magnified 700 diameters
we see the several points represented in Fig. 1, pl. I.
In every one of those oval masses of bioplasm coloured
red, vital phenomena occurred during life.   The
physicist and chemist are utterly unable to explain
the actions going on in the bioplasts, or to tell us
exactly what sort of changes occur, or in what way
the nutrient matter, taken up from the blood, is
changed and some of its elements re-arranged, so that
at length is produced the firm tissue on which the
physical properties of the texture in question entirely
depend.

After careful study of such a specimen, we may
form a notion of the manner in which the bioplasm
divides and subdivides, and becomes resolved into
formed material which accumulates upon its surface,
and eventually hardens and constitutes an effective
protection to the delicate textures which lie beneath

it. We can also understand how the new elementary parts gradually grow up from beneath and supply the place of the old ones which are cast off from the free surface. But these phenomena cannot be explained by physics and chemistry, or without calling in the aid of the hypothesis of vital power.

Bone of Kitten and its Bioplasm.—Next, let us ascertain whether the examination of other tissues in the body teaches us the same general facts. In Pl. II, fig. 1, p. 46, is represented a small piece of the permanent bone with the subjacent soft texture of a kitten at birth. To the left is the delicate growing tissue in which the vessels that have been artificially injected with Prussian-blue are distributed. From the blood circulating in these all the elements entering into the formation of bone are selected. The little bioplasts above *c* are the agents actively concerned in the operation. These take up nutrient matter, and grow and multiply, and become separated further and further from one another as the delicate tissue which they form increases in the intervals between them. The matrix thus produced afterwards becomes the seat of deposition of calcareous salts, in consequence, probably, of chemical changes, *d*. The calcareous salts become incorporated with the organic matrix, and the bone formation is complete, *c*. The process continues, but more slowly, until each little bioplast henceforth drawing its nutrient material through pores (canaliculi), left during the progress of the

every one of these different tissues are minute masses of *living matter* or *bioplasm*. The matter of which the several bioplasts taking part in the formation of all these very different tissues are composed, possesses the same characters, although the several forms of bioplasm produce tissues differing from one another in the most essential particulars.

At an earlier period of life, the little tissue-forming bioplasts were situated much nearer to one another. This separation of the bioplasts is a necessary consequence of the formation of formed material or tissue, which proceeds, and, as age advances, accumulates in the intervals between the bioplasts. At a still earlier period the bioplasts, which were to take part in the formation of cuticle, nerves, vessels, pigment-cells, fibrous tissue, &c., respectively, were quite close together, or formed part of one bioplasm-mass.

It would have been impossible had the tissue been examined at an early period, to determine which was a *nerve bioplast*, which a *pigment bioplast*, and which was to take part in the formation of a *vessel*, or at length to assume the form of a *blood corpuscle*. But all these bioplasts have descended from a common bioplasmic mass. It is absurd, therefore, to attempt to explain the results, as some have done, by affirming that they are due to *differentiation*, to *molecular changes*, or to machinery, or to *physical influences*, for it must be obvious that by these phrases no explanation whatever is afforded.

The bioplasm of an advanced tissue cannot be distinguished from embryonic bioplasm any more than the bioplasm of one tissue can be distinguished from that of another. That there must be a vast difference in power is certain, from the very different results which are brought about. The difference between bioplasts is not a difference in physical characters, or in structure, or in chemical properties, nor is it to be expressed in force terms. Physical authorities may assert that the difference is due to some difference in the " molecular changes " which take place, but then we must inquire what occasions the difference ? Moreover, since nothing is known as regards the supposed molecular changes, while the meaning of the term " molecular," as it is employed here, cannot be defined, it is obvious that the announcement amounts to absolutely nothing more than the admission that a change occurs, but that nothing whatever is known to physicists concerning its nature, and nothing is known of the circumstances which determine its occurrence.

No one who studies such a tissue as this will feel at all satisfied with the manner in which its description is dismissed by many of those who have not the patience or inclination to pursue microscopical investigation, and who endeavour to prejudice persons against minute inquiries and the facts which have been demonstrated thereby.*

* The most positive assertions have been made concerning facts only to be demonstrated and understood by those who have made themselves

It is very significant that no attempt is made by philosophers who discourse on the origin and destination of living beings and of the world they inhabit, to account for the wonderful arrangement of one of the very many textures of a living thing, and of the intimate relationship they bear to one another, or for their exquisite and orderly adaptation by which excellence of action and perfect fulfilment of the objects of their formation are ensured.

A nerve centre is represented in Fig. 1, pl. III. The little oval bodies embedded in it are the *nerve cells*, from each of which two or more delicate nerve fibres extend, or have been drawn out during the growth of the tissue. These nerve fibres run between contiguous cells and seem to surround them, as in the drawing. Formerly they were supposed to form a capsule of "connective tissue," in which it was said the nerve cells were embedded.

The 'cells' are the sources of nerve force, which is, perhaps, closely allied to, but more probably identical with electricity. The currents starting from a cell traverse nerve fibres, which are often of great length, and, after being conducted along many fine fibres resulting from subdivision of the original nerve fibre,

practically familiar with minute inquiry, by authorities who have been occupied in a totally distinct branch of scientific investigation, and who are quite ignorant of microscopical work. Microscopical observers have been told what they ought to have seen, and what they have seen has been condemned by 'philosophers' whose remarks prove them to be absolutely ignorant even of the first principles of observation.

E

probably at length return to the same cell. Thus there are in every part of the nervous system excessively delicate fibres or cords forming continuous tracts. These constitute complete circuits, in various parts of which are situated the organs which are under the control and government of the nerve centres, Pl. II, fig. 2.

Nerve fibres are the cords which transmit the nerve force, and there has been much discussion concerning the character of the material which plays this very important part, and the changes which supervene when it is thrown into a state of activity. Attempts have been made to discover some peculiar structure or constitution of the active part of the nerve fibre, which will enable us to explain its action. Many very positive but very fanciful assertions have unfortunately had the effect of leading us away from the truth, and have encouraged the general acceptance of erroneous hypotheses in cases where a little consideration of the actual facts might have led to the adoption of a correct conclusion.

It has been assumed that the active part of the nerve fibre (the axis cylinder) is composed of some *peculiar colloid*. Had Mr. Herbert Spencer examined the axis cylinders of some nerves, he would have found that the material of which they were composed very closely resembled some kinds of ordinary fibrous tissue. Of course it may be said, "that this resemblance does not prove identity, either of structure or composition." And it has been argued, that we must not draw conclusions from positive observations, because beyond the limit of observation there *may be* facts which, if they could be ascertained, might justify conclusions at variance with those deduced from the facts we have. But there is nothing to be demonstrated by investigation to justify the conclusion that the *action* of the axis cylinder is due to any special peculiarity of structure or composition. The axis cylinder is composed of " protein substance," says Mr. Spencer, but this is not a peculiarity, since a number of tissues may be said with equal truth to consist of protein substance. It has been affirmed that the peculiar colloid " habitually changed from one of its *isomeric states* to another ;" but in this particular it would be difficult to prove that it differed from many other things. There is no more reason for supposing that the axis cylinder consists of " matter isomerically transformed with ease," than that white or yellow fibrous tissue consists of such material. Nor is there any reason whatever for assuming that a continuous length of fibrous tissue, or even moist thread, would not be an efficient medium for the transmission of nerve force, if it were protected and arranged like the axis cylinder of a nerve. It is very curious to notice the indignation of some philosophers if anyone speaks of vital power, while they themselves, in the most innocent manner, assume the discovery of peculiar colloids and matters isomerically transformed with ease to suit the terms of any physical proposition which they feel disposed to propound. The attempt to show that a nerve is formed by physical changes, and acts by virtue of some peculiar chemical properties, has not succeeded.

Of the Fine Nerve Fibres around an Artery.—The degree of contraction of the muscular fibres encircling every little branch of an artery, as represented in Fig. 2, is constantly varying, and this change is determined by the varying intensity of the current traversing the nerves distributed to the muscular coat. Any alteration in the calibre of the artery instantly affects the flow of blood through the vessel, and a greater or less quantity of blood is distributed to the capillaries in a given time, according as the arterial coat is contracted or relaxed. In this way, through the intervention of a highly complex mechanism, the nerve centres exert an indirect but very important regulating influence upon the process of nutrition.

Distributed immediately external to the *capillary vessels*, are also very fine nerve fibres, branches of which join the network around the arteries. These nerve fibres of the capillaries are probably connected with the same nerve centres, and, perhaps, with the same cells as those from which the nerves distributed to the artery emanate. There results by this arrangement a very elaborate self-regulating mechanism of wonderful perfection, by which the supply of nutrient material to the tissues and organs of vertebrate animals is regulated according to the demand, and is

X 130

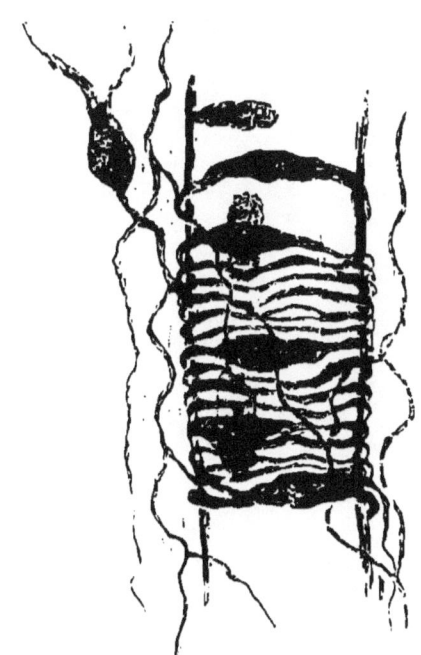

of a ganglion on the nerve. Shows
the side of a nerve, showing gan-
on the nerve fibres around them, which
the trunk and are there distributed
to the nerves of the periradium of
the x   X 130, p

portion of very small arteries in the
ar fibre cells and nerve fibres ramifying
the areolar coat. Brat   X 700. p. 3.

113.

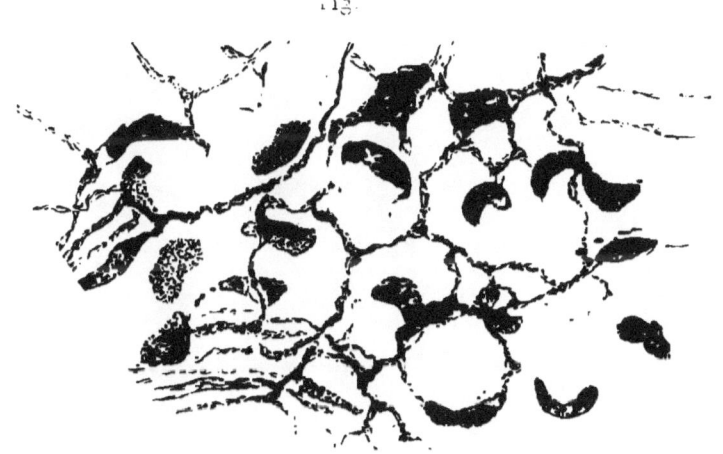

altered according as the conditions to which the tissues themselves are exposed as regards heat, moisture, and the like, undergo change. But into the consideration of this subject, interesting and important though it undoubtedly is, as an illustration of the existence of arrangements which cannot be brought about by material changes alone, I must not further enter now.

Capillaries and Nerve Fibres, Palate of the Frog.— In Fig. 3, pl. III, is represented a small capillary vessel from the mucous membrane of the palate of the frog. These capillaries exhibit at short intervals little pouches or diverticula, the use of which has not been fully explained, but which probably act as little reservoirs in which the blood remains partially stagnant, so that the exudation of fluid from it for the nutrition of rapidly-growing epithelium is favoured. It must be obvious, from the position of the numerous nerve fibres seen around the capillaries, that very slight increase in the diameter of a vessel, consequent upon its distension by blood, would affect the nerve fibres ramifying upon its exterior. In consequence an influence would be produced upon the nerve centre which would be immediately followed by the conveyance of an impulse along the nerves distributed to the artery (p. 52). Contraction of the little arteries distributing blood to the capillaries involved, would follow, and a reduced flow of blood through the capillaries would be occasioned.

Vessels and Nerve Fibres of Mucous Membrane.—In Fig. 1, pl. IV, is a representation of a very interesting specimen, from which the reader may gain an idea of the multitudes of bioplasts which exist in connection with some of the sensitive textures of man. The drawing represents a thin section of the mucous membrane of the human epiglottis of man immediately beneath the epithelium. Numerous bundles of delicate nerve fibres are seen ramifying in all directions, and interlacing freely with one another. Bioplasts are observed in connection with the nerve fibres. The majority of the nerves represented, probably take part in sensation, but a few of the finest fibres may be traced to the capillary vessels. Before the physical theory of life can be accepted, it must be shown how, according to that doctrine, the arrangement of the nerve fibres demonstrated in such a specimen may be accounted for.

Large Caudate Nerve Cells.—In the great central organs of the cerebro-spinal system of man, and the higher vertebrata, the elementary parts or cells are very large, and of an irregular form. These are the so-called *caudate nerve vesicles*, which should, I think, be regarded as stations where numerous nerve tracts cross and intersect, and then pass off from the "cell" in various directions, Pl. IV, fig. 2.

The bioplasm which takes part in the formation of these complex organs is situated near the central part of the cell. The so-called "nucleus," that is the

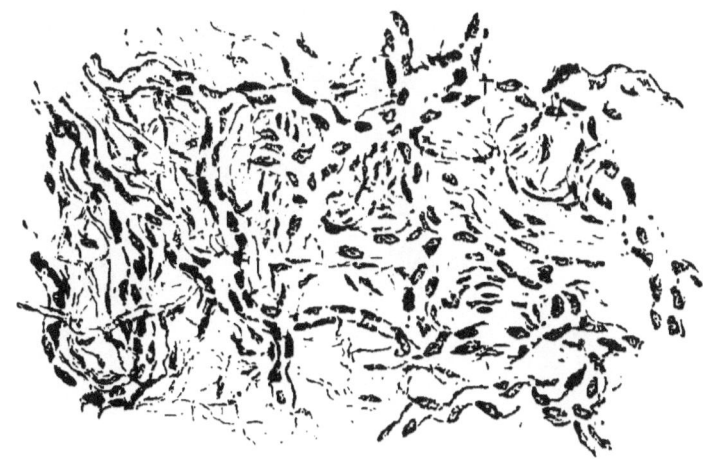

Muc...is m...mbrane cov...ring th...ep...s, h...man s...b...t...d... ...t...s
...en...ath the ej...th li...m. Tbe...a...ı...ar...s...with th...r...n...ss s... ...ısoı...e
ın the...ınterv...ls are seen...numer...ıs...bun...ı...s of n...rve fibr... ...   ...t...ı...ıst
...re, h...wever, far too d...ıc...te to be se...ı...n a spe...ım...n...ı...   ...l...ı...ıd...m...ı

Fı...

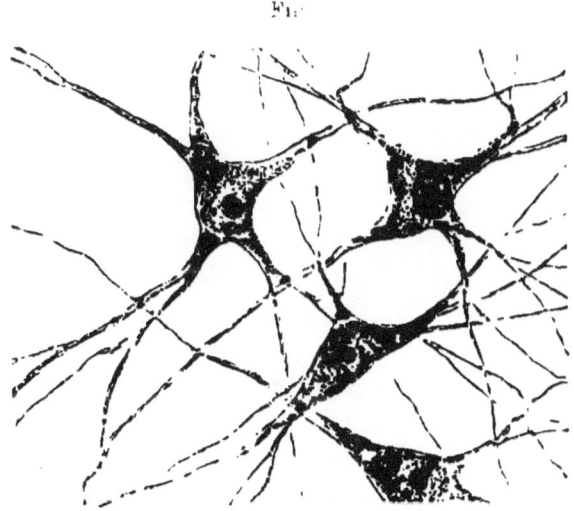

Anı...ın ard...nd...ı...n...ve... ...ı...ı ...ı...ı...ı...ı...ı...ı...ı... ...ı... ...ı...ı...ı...ı)
ı...ı...ı...ı...ı...ı...ı...ı...ı...ı...ı...ı...ı...ı...ı...ı...ı...ı...ı

inner part of the bioplasm or living matter of the cell, is not connected with the nerve fibres as some have supposed, but it is concerned in the formation of the soft material which constitutes the body of the cell, and which is traversed by the nerve currents as these course across the cell from one fibre to the others which leave it.

Cells of the Grey Matter of the Convolutions of the Brain.—Caudate nerve-cells, smaller than those from the spinal cord, just referred to, but of the same type of structure, are found in other parts of the cerebro-spinal centres. In the grey matter of the brain they are very numerous. In fact the greater part of this structure is made up of these cells, and extremely delicate nerve fibres ramifying amongst them. Many of the cells are remarkable for tapering into one ex-cessively long fibre, which becomes very fine, and proceeds in a direction towards the surface of the brain. This fibre passes some distance before it divides into its finest ramifications. The fibres from the base of the cell, however, divide and subdivide into numerous branches as soon as they have left it. The arrangement is figured in 2 and 3, Plate V.

If the reader will carefully examine Fig. 3, he will be able to form some conception of the vast multitudes of these cells in the grey matter of the brain of one of the lower animals (the Guinea pig). The piece represented is really not so large as the head of a very small pin, and is very thin,—much thinner than the thinnest

tissue paper. In a piece of grey matter of the size
of a mustard-seed, there would be many thousands of
such cells, and the space of one cubic inch would
contain several millions. The relation and arrangement of the vessels are also well seen in the drawing
under consideration. Occupying every portion of the
intervals between the cells, are multitudes of fibres
which it is impossible to give in the drawing. A very
imperfect idea of the arrangement may, however, be
formed from the representation given in the lower
part of Fig. 1, pl. V, to the left. These fibres all come
from cells, and each is in fact composed of numerous
tracts along which nerve-currents pass. At each cell
many different circuits intersect, and in this way lines
are established between many distant parts and organs
situated far from one another. These may all be
influenced, and at the same moment of time, by
changes occurring in one part of a single nerve circuit ;
and complex movements of groups of muscles placed
at great distances from one another and from their
nervous centre, may be executed, and very different
and distinct actions combined and harmonized most
perfectly, and at the same instant.

Is it right that authorities in other departments of
knowledge, who are perfectly ignorant of these marvellous arrangements, and lack the disposition to learn
facts that others could teach them, having neither
patience nor skill to examine the textures for themselves and make out their structure, should assert

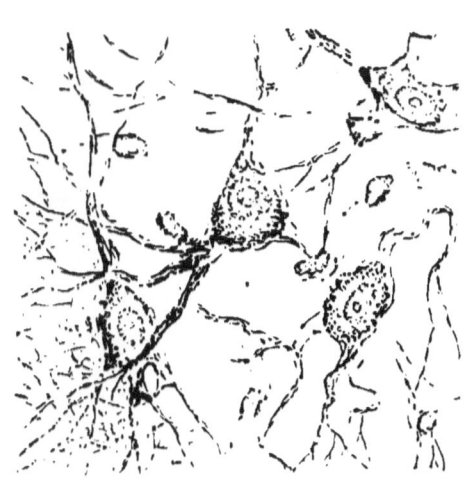

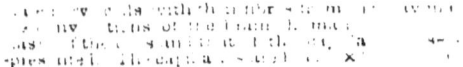

Fig.

most positively, and teach far and wide, that the whole of this marvellous mechanism was built by the sun and constructed by force? But it is wonderful that the public should accept such assertions without question, and even delight in being told again and again that the brain is a force-constructed mind-evolving mill. The philosophers in question are, of course, unable to tell us how a single cell is formed, or how the wonderfully complex interlacement of fibres, which exists everywhere, is effected. They do not inquire how the fibre grows from the cell, and are uncertain whether, indeed, the processes of the cell are prolonged into nerve fibres or not. And numerous other structural matters of fundamental importance seem to be equally beneath their notice. They have decided to their own satisfaction what the nerve tissue is, or what it ought to be; how it ought to act, and how it ought to have been formed, and according to them there is an end of the matter materially.

I am sorry again to criticise Mr. Herbert Spencer's statement of facts, but the description given by him of the formation of nerve cells and fibres is in many respects so vague and incorrect, that it ought not to be allowed to pass. He says, "the vesicles or corpuscles *appear to take their rise* out of a nitrogenous protoplasm, *full* of *granules,** and

---

* The granules, it is said, consist of "fatty matter," but how they came to be we are not told.

containing *nuclei.*" Now, every tissue in the body
may be said to take its rise out of a nitrogenous
protoplasm, so that such an assertion conveys absolutely no information respecting the formation of
nerve cells. What the "*granules*" may be Mr. Spencer does not tell us, nor does he consider it necessary
to account for the origin of the nitrogenous protoplasm, or to describe the nature and properties of this
particular nerve-corpuscle-forming matter. Round
these nuclei, he goes on to remark, "the protoplasm
aggregates into spheroidal masses, which, becoming
severally inclosed in delicate membranes (in many
cases inferred rather than seen) *are so made into nerve
cells !*" Now, this statement is altogether unsup-
ported by observation ; it is, indeed, positively incorrect. The protoplasm does not aggregate at all,
the masses are not severally enclosed in delicate
membrane, and nerve cells are not made in the
manner described. Further on, it is affirmed that
the "nucleated cells, or nerve-corpuscles, *give off*
processes ;" but how they "give off" processes, or
what makes them give off processes, we are not
told. But the processes are not formed by being
"given off" from the cells in any case, as far as is
known. The cells which were originally connected
move away from one another, and the process or in-
tervening fibre is as it were drawn off from them. It
is evident from his description, that Mr. Herbert
Spencer has but a very imperfect notion of the struc-

tures he describes, and has not seen them. If he has examined specimens, they must have been very imperfect, or the method of conducting the examination faulty.

In explaining nerve action, Mr. Herbert Spencer seems to consider that the active part of the nerve fibre is protoplasm, and the material out of which the nerve fibre is formed is, according to him, also protoplasm ; but these two kinds of "protoplasm" are as distinct from one another as the moving, living, growing protoplasm of the white blood corpuscle is from the stationary, firm, solid, passive white or yellow fibrous tissue. Things so very different, should be described differently, and cannot be supposed to act alike.

The tissue, moreover, never "builds up." It is the particles of the matter, while in the living state which "build up," and arrange themselves, or are arranged by some force or power active in this temporary exceptional (living) condition. The assertion that "among the corpuscles and their branches are distributed the *terminations* of nerve fibres" is another error, for no terminations whatever have been demonstrated by anyone in any nerve-centre. Neither is it true that in any nervous centre "the connections between fibres and cells are rarely, if ever, direct." I have introduced these criticisms to show that many of the so-called *facts* upon which certain conjectural views have been based are only facts of the imagination of privileged persons.

But I will not pursue this subject more in detail in this place, as my object in referring to the structure of tissues is only to direct attention to the living matter, which has been completely ignored by many physical philosophers, but is nevertheless to be demonstrated in connection with all the tissues of man and animals, and from which everything in their bodies has been formed.

· Before leaving this part of my subject, however, I must say a few words upon the elementary parts of the brain, which are, I believe, the bioplasts immediately concerned in the active operations of the mind These are situated in the soft grey matter which forms the convolutions of brain, consisting of an enormously extended thin layer, so folded as to occupy the least possible space.

Bioplasm concerned in Mental Nerve Action.*—Near the surface of the grey matter in that extensive layer above the planes in which the caudate nerve-cells are situated, which is generally said to be composed of delicate nerve fibres and "granular matter," I have succeeded in demonstrating multitudes of very small masses of bioplasm lying amongst the finest branches of the nerve fibres, something like those which constitute the so-called "granular layer" of the retina and of the cerebellum. In some places there are aggregations or collections of these bodies. They are

---

* The following description is taken from "Protoplasm," but the plate illustrating these remarks is new.

nearly spherical, are extremely delicate, and become disintegrated very soon after death. Some sections of grey matter appear to consist almost entirely of these bodies, so great is their number. Some seem to be connected together by very delicate processes of the same transparent material.

Masses of bioplasm thus situated are arranged very favourably for influencing the fine nerve fibres which ramify amongst them, Figs. 1 and 2, pl. VI, p. 62. It is obvious that the slightest change in their form could not fail to affect the nerve currents traversing these fibres, and as we are now well acquainted with the active movements of bioplasm, it is impossible to help suggesting that the movements occurring in these masses of living matter produce a direct effect upon the adjacent fibres. These *vital* movements or vibrations occurring in matter of excessive tenuity constitute, or are the immediate consequences of mental vital action. The directions in which the living matter is made to move by the conscious life-power which directs it, will determine the particular cords of the nerve mechanism to be struck; the special movements may be the expressions of the inward ideas. If this be so, mind is the *vital power* which is associated with this the most exalted form of living or germinal matter, so arranged that the slightest change occurring in it may produce indirectly an effect through the influence of a most elaborate mechanism, brought into very intimate relation with

it.   Does any one, who has studied structure, really
believe that through physics or chemistry the slightest
approach to an explanation of the formation of the
mechanism or of its action will ever be made ?

The conclusion that will be drawn from the facts
ascertained by a careful examination of the several
preparations just described (and almost any others
prepared like these would have equally answered my
purpose), is that the physical doctrine of life appears
plausible only if the facts of nature are regarded very
cursorily and superficially.   As we investigate more
minutely we find that difficulties present themselves to
this physical interpretation of the facts, and these
difficulties increase in number at every step.   If we
employ the highest powers, and so prepare the tissues
that the delicate structure is very slightly deranged,
we see great reason to demur to the acceptance of the
physical doctrine of life.   While, if we investigate
the distribution of the bioplasm, study its arrangement and relation to the different tissues at different
periods of life, and submit living bioplasm under
favourable circumstances to the magnifying power of
from 1,500 to 3,000 diameters, the conviction will force
itself upon the mind that any attempt to explain by
physics the phenomena we demonstrate must utterly
fail at this time.

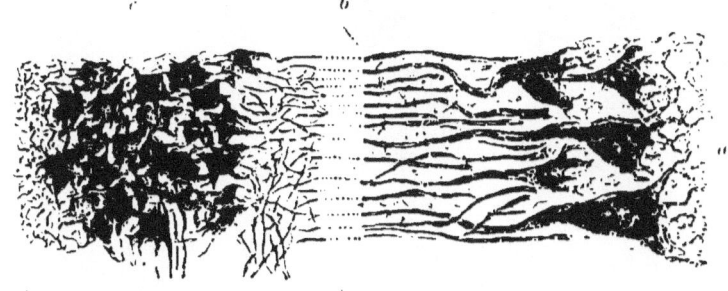

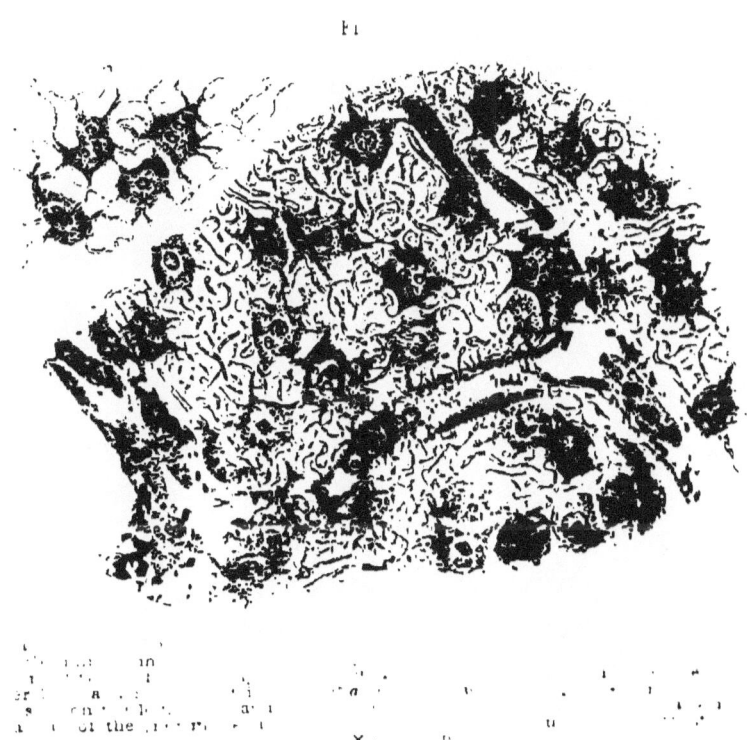

We may now consider some of the *vital phenomena* which are common to every form of *bioplasm* in nature, from the lowest and simplest to the very highest.

Characters of the Bioplasm.—The living matter has been proved by the aid of higher magnifying powers than had been used before 1863, to be clear, transparent, and *structureless*. I have shown that the phenomena of growth, nutrition, and multiplication could not be explained by any structural or mechanical arrangements. No structure of any kind can be seen, even when the bioplasm is magnified 5,000 diameters.* The remarkable fact was demonstrated that a minute portion of transparent, colourless, living matter exhibited very peculiar movements—movements which could not be explained by any known laws. One part of the bioplasm could be seen to move in advance of another part, or over it, as it were, or through it, just as if the mass of living matter consisted of colourless fluid, every particle of which had the capacity of movement, and at the same time. One part could be seen to move, as it were, into or through another part, in one case blending partially or completely, in another apparently remaining distinct from the rest.

* "On the Structure and Growth of the Tissues," a course of lectures delivered at the Royal College of Physicians, April and May, 1861.

The bioplasm embedded in a tissue (pages 44, 45) does not pass gradually into the formed matter, as some have asserted, but the transition is sudden and abrupt. The living appears to be in contact with that which has ceased to live. In a given bulk of the matter of the different tissues of the living body and at different ages, the relative proportion of the living to the lifeless matter varies greatly (Plate I) ; but every little particle of bioplasm has upon its surface, in contact with it, lifeless matter, which may be very sparing in quantity, as in quickly growing tissues, or constitute by far the largest part of the matter.

This living matter is intimately concerned in the *growth, nutrition*, and *action* of every texture of every living being, animal, or vegetable, as long as it remains alive. Towards every one of the minute masses of bioplasm represented in the Plates in this volume, currents of fluid, holding nutrient matters in solution, flowed during life. In this way every portion of the surrounding tissue, it will be observed, must have been continually bathed with fresh fluid, and thus it was preserved in a state favourable for the discharge of its function. Nor is it possible to explain any of these processes without taking into account the phenomena of the living matter. If the living matter dies, these processes at once stop. A particle of matter cannot, I think, be either half alive or half dead. It must be living, or it must absolutely have ceased to live. When we study a thing that is alive, we do not find that every particle of the matter of the being lives, but that only the *bioplasm* of its organism is actually living. This only can grow and take up nourishment and convert and multiply.

And if we study the ordinary phenomena of living beings, we shall find that they may be traced to their antecedent phenomena, through perhaps a long chain, until at last we arrive at the really *vital phenomena* of the bioplasm or living matter. But at this point our investigation for the present must stop. For let us suppose that a most skilful chemist sets to work to ascertain what this living matter is made of. Ere his chemical analysis can commence the matter has passed from the living state, and all that he can do is to ascertain the nature of the chemical substances which are formed when it dies and after its death. The chemical composition of living matter is unknown and probably unknowable, for it is impossible to analyse matter that is *living*. To assert therefore that living matter is " protein " or " albumen " is to assert that which never has been and never can be proved, and all arguments based upon such assertions must be discarded. To say that living matter consists of these things *changed* or *modified* is mere evasion, and any physiologist who adopts this expedient evades the consideration of the question, for of the chemistry of the *living matter itself*, and of the manner in which the chemical changes are effected, he is aware that he knows nothing.

F

and that nothing is really known. No one has been able to give any explanation of the phenomena regarded from the physical point of view. We can all of us see living matter move, see one part raising itself above and in advance of another part, in spite of the action of gravitation ; but the most delicate refinements of physical research have so far failed to help us to discover the nature or cause of the movement, or even to afford any conception of the exact changes which occur while the movements are going on under our eyes. The assertion that the movement is *molecular* and a consequence of previous *molecular changes* is mere pretence of knowledge, for, as before stated, nothing whatever is known of the *molecular* phenomena supposed, or of the changes which give rise to these. So far therefore it is right to regard the distinction between the living and the non-living as *absolute,* and all hypotheses which are based upon the idea that this difference is one of degree only and that vital power is but a mode of ordinary force must be abandoned, although no doubt physical views of life will yet be urged upon the attention of unlearned people. Observers who are acquainted with the facts and are able to investigate details will condemn them because they are opposed to reason and calculated only to mislead the ignorant.

Those who seek to explain vital actions by attributing them to antecedent changes, are in a somewhat better position than those who assert the changes to be actually molecular, although this view is also un-tenable. The doctrine under consideration rests upon the idea of the dependence of every change upon an antecedent change. But who can tell us anything concerning the nature of the change antecedent to the changes which can be observed in living matter? As yet we have no means of following up the inquiry one step beyond the observed change. It comes then to this: that the physical doctrine at this time rests upon the *assertion* that the phenomena of living matter are of the same order and nature as the phe-nomena of non-living matter. There are absolutely no facts to which the advocates of this doctrine can appeal in support of their conclusion. Analytical operations do not enable us to learn anything con-cerning the changes of the actual bioplasm or *living matter.* Neither physicists, chemists, nor any other scientific investigators can explain to us the nature of the changes which occur in it. We know of the phenomena, but to account for them by any laws of nature now known is not possible, and it is surely presumptuous, instead of being philosophical, on the part of any one to permit himself to assert dogmati-cally that the changes must be *physical* and due to the operation of the same laws which affect non-living matter, because all change is physical and all laws are physical laws.

Nutrition.—Living matter, if placed under certain conditions as regards temperature, moisture, and light, and at the same time surrounded by fluid holding in solution certain compounds, increases in amount. The matter which is added and which becomes part of the mass cannot after its incorporation be distinguished from the rest. In other words, the living matter takes up non-living matter and converts this into living matter. This is nutrition.

It is generally supposed that this process of nutrition goes on in every particle of *tissue*,—that, for example, the fibrous tissue *selects* from the blood constituents which become fibrous tissue,—that in the same way muscle and nerve and other textures select the proper materials adapted for their increase. But this is not so. The *tissues* have no such selecting or metabolic properties. The bioplasm only possesses the marvellous power of taking into itself certain matters, and of changing them in such a manner, and at length of undergoing conversion into tissue. Without bioplasm there can be neither *nutrition*, nor *growth*, nor *development*, nor *tissue-formation* of any kind.

But further, when a mass of living matter is freely supplied with pabulum instead of increasing indefinitely, it attains a certain size and then undergoes division. In this way the number of masses of bioplasm increase during the period of development and early life. In many parts of the body this increase continues while life lasts, but the growth and multiplication of different forms of bioplasm of the body, and of the same form at different ages take place at a very different rate. These, like other phenomena of the bioplasm, are inexplicable by physics, and all conclusions concerning the nature of growth, nutrition, and increase which rest upon the assumption that these phenomena are physical and chemical are unsound, illogical, and misleading. Such views retard progress and tend to prevent the spread of natural knowledge.

Bioplasm in Disease.—The bioplasm or living matter circulating in the fluids and embedded in the textures of the body undergoes most important changes in disease. Oftentimes it increases to many times the volume it occupied in the healthy state, and thus the most terrible derangement of many physiological processes may be occasioned, and in several ways. In every form of fever and inflammation the bioplasm increases, and its increase is associated with the development of heat. Living matter or bioplasm constitutes those minute particles known as *disease germs*, which are the agents concerned in propagating all contagious diseases.* Having escaped from the infected organism, the particles of contagious bioplasm, often less than the $\frac{1}{100000}$ of an inch in diameter, may be wafted by currents of air, perhaps through very considerable distances. If any of them accidentally come in contact with an organism in a state favourable to their growth and multiplication, they may pass into the blood, grow and multiply, and establish a state of

* See " Disease Germs, their Real Nature." January, 1871.

disease like that existing in the organism whence they were derived. It need scarcely be observed that the changes of bioplasm in disease are not to be explained by mechanics or chemistry.

Production of Formed Material from Bioplasm.— Not less wonderful than the other vital phenomena to which I have adverted is the following, which occurs whenever tissue of any kind is formed.

A mass of living matter undergoes change upon its surface. Some of the living material loses its *vital* powers, it ceases to be nourished, and ceases to grow. Part of the living bioplasm in fact ceases to live. It dies and is changed. The elements of which it consists are rearranged, and thus lifeless formed material and non-living tissues of every kind result.

Many of those most beautiful and transparent jelly-like creatures known as animalcules, which exhibit such wonderful activity in warm weather, become torpid and perfectly quiescent when exposed to cold. If they be examined in winter, it will be found that the beautiful transparent textures have become granular, and highly refracting insoluble particles can sometimes be detected in considerable number. These changes result from the death of part of the living matter of which these delicate organisms were in great part composed. By the accumulation of dead matter (cell-wall) upon the surface of the bioplasm, what remains of this is protected and saved from death. When spring returns and external conditions become favourable to growth, many of the lifeless granules are cast away, and the living matter escapes from the dead capsules, or much of the dead matter may be taken up by the little bioplasm which remained in a living state. This then rapidly increases, and a mass of living matter having the characteristic transparency and delicacy of appearance soon results. Changes of the same kind occur in bioplasts of all living things under certain alterations of the conditions under which they grow and live.

Bioplasm and Formed Matter.—The passive formed material around the bioplasm *has resulted from changes in the bioplasm itself. Formed material cannot form.* Formed material is as different from the living matter as the wood of the table from the living growing tree. Some advocates of the physical theory of life call these two different kinds of matter by the very same name, and in this way they seek to make people believe that there is no real absolute difference between the two—between that which *lives* and that which has *lived*. Matter in these two very different forms or states has been called by the same name, protoplasm. But even Mr. Huxley is obliged to acknowledge that there is a difference, although he has succeeded in hiding it for a time by the ingenious device of telling people that the protoplasm is " *variously modified !* " And he informs his readers by what forces the modification is effected. He says the matter is modified by " subtle influences."

According to the present philosophy, the *living* is
but modified *lifeless.* The watch then is but the
modified brass or steel. Grass is but *modified* earth,
man only *modified* dust. And the conversion of the
lifeless into the living, of the metals into the watch, of
the earth into the grass, and of the dust into man, is
effected not by any immaterial agents whatever—not
by such fictions as vitality, but by tangible demon-
strable, accurately defined means which physical
philosophers can render evident to the senses of
privileged persons, and which pass by the names of
" conditions," " circumstances," and " subtle influences."

At no previous period in the history of science have
such poor attempts to palm off as an explanation that
which is but an assertion, been so successful. Never
before have people been led to accept as explanations
such phrases as " variously modified." Anyone
accustomed to analyse the meaning of terms though
he possessed no scientific information whatever, could,
with very little trouble, resolve such explanations into
mere wind and words, but unfortunately in these days
people will not take trouble, and are too busy to study,
to analyse, to weigh, to reflect,—and more respect is
excited by the dress in which observations and arguments are clothed, than by the observations and
arguments themselves.

*Objections to the Idea of a Central Force or Power
influencing the whole Organism.*—Some have enter-

tained the idea that the phenomena of the organism of man and the higher animals, can only be accounted for by admitting the action for some *central* guiding, directing power, capable of influencing all the organs and tissues of the body in somewhat the same way as the master builder controls and directs the operations of his workmen. To such hypothetical influences have been attributed many complex phenomena not easily accounted for. But there is no good reason for believing that any such central mysterious presiding unity, force, property, or agency exists in some one part of the body, and from the first dawn of life influences regulates or controls the numerous and highly complex phenomena simultaneously occurring in every part of the living being. Regularity of growth, Development of structure, Maintenance of nutrition, and Harmony of action, can be otherwise accounted for. It is therefore unnecessary to resort to an hypothesis which involves the untenable doctrine that lifeless tissue in the body is influenced by some apocryphal central force which commands it, which effects changes, governs by some undiscovered laws, and operates in some at present inconceivable manner and in many different directions through different kinds of matter, and at very varying distances at the same instant. There is no better reason for assuming " life" to be located in one central spot, than for the old view that it was established in the blood, and was distributed elsewhere by this fluid.

The evidence I have advanced is, I think, conclusive in showing that the only *life* in the body is associated with bioplasm, some of which is to be found in every tissue and organ in every part of the body and in the blood at every period of life. The only particles capable of being influenced by *vitality* are those which are actually living ; in fact, the matter of which the bioplasm itself consists.

But the different forms of bioplasm which are concerned in the formation of different tissues and organs of the body, possess special *vital* powers. The marvellous manifestation of vital power by which man is so widely separated from all other beings, does not emanate from the bioplasm of the tissues generally, but is limited to that of one special tissue. Neither the bioplasm of bone nor that of muscle nor skin, nor that which takes part in the formation of glands, is the seat of those phenomena which absolutely separate man from every other being in nature. There is no reason to suppose that man's bone and muscle, skin or glands, are in any essential points very different from the corresponding structures in the lower animals. But the particular kind of bioplasm which takes part in intellectual action resides in the brain of man alone. Between this and every other form of bioplasm in man's body and elsewhere, there is a transcendant difference, not, however, in the matter of which it is composed, but as regards the power with which it is endowed.

The bioplasm of all the different tissues of the body has been derived by descent from one mass of bioplasm. After the bioplasts have once been detached, they do not probably exert any direct influence upon one another. That bioplasts with certain special endowments or properties, eventually result by division from the original bioplasm is certain, but neither this fact nor the sort of power manifested, could have been premised, however carefully the original mass of bioplasm had been examined. No knowledge of the properties, characters, or composition of the matter would have enabled us to form any conception of the nature of the actions it was to perform.

It has been supposed by some that a central force operates on the distant parts of the body through the nervous system, but it is certain that neither the arrangement of the tissues to form organs having special functions, nor their actions, can be accounted for by any governing or directing agency brought to bear through the intervention of nerve. Indeed, this tissue is not developed at the time the arrangements in question are determined and carried into effect. The nervous system, instead of being developed first, as it undoubtedly would be if it was to exercise the function supposed, arrives at maturity the very last of all the tissues. The highest form of bioplasm developed, and the only one which could be supposed with any show of reason to exercise sway over all the rest, and over the various tissues formed, is the

very last to appear in the order of development, and
is not in action until long after many of the changes
supposed to be due to some central force or power
have been completed.

To this, the last produced, every other form of bioplasm appears to be in a manner subordinate. Other
forms seem to have been called into being in order
that this might exist. The tissues and organs,
ministering to the well-being of this highest form, are
perhaps not necessary to its actual existence, but are
required for preserving it in a state of integrity,
while some are employed as the instruments through
which alone such a power can express itself, and be
brought into relation with, or produce any effect
upon the non-living matter around it.

There is then no reason for adopting the conclusion
that the several tissues and organs which constitute
an organism are under the influence of any central
power capable of exerting any general control upon
all ; but after a careful examination of the facts ascertained during the course of development and formation of a tissue, the inference is deduced that each
tissue is formed by living matter, which exerts no
direct action or controlling influence upon the living
matter of other and different tissues. Nor do the
particles of living matter of the same tissue exert
any direct influence upon one another. A long series
of changes occurring in regular pre-ordained order,
results at last in the complete development of a

texture. If, after development is completed, the various conditions which have themselves in great part resulted from the occurrence of previous developmental (vital) changes, are not disturbed, the growth and action of the tissues is preserved. But derangement of any one organ may interfere with the proper action of others, either by influencing the composition of the nutrient matter distributed to all, or by disturbing the action of the nerves which supply them.

Vital Phenomena and Physical Phenomena of a Different Order.—But it has been shown that the phenomena of living matter are quite peculiar, and are limited to the living matter which has been detached from a mass of matter that was alive. A wide distinction, therefore, ought to be drawn between the *vital phenomena* occurring in living matter and the *physical* and *chemical phenomena* of the non-living matter of living beings. The living is altogether different from the non-living, and the former in no way involves the existence of the latter (page 10). In all living beings there are indeed two distinct sets of phenomena, *vital* and *physico-chemical.* The vital phenomena exhibit no analogy whatever to the physico-chemical phenomena. The physical properties of the molecules are no more capable of being lost than the molecules themselves, but the vital properties may disappear and never again be manifested by the same particular molecules.

It must, however, be acknowledged that we are not able to adduce scientific evidence in proof that the *living* can exist independently of the *non-living*, because the only evidence obtainable by us is obtained from and through the material. Such a conception, however, may present itself to the mind, and it seems not unreasonable to believe that *vitality* may after all belong to an order of *activities* or *immaterial agents* of which we can really learn nothing directly by the assistance of our senses. Nevertheless, from the effects of the supposed agency upon matter, we can conceive of it as an actual existing power, and by studying accurately the results of its working, why should we not succeed in drawing a correct conclusion concerning its nature and the mode of its action upon matter ?

Vitality.—The *vital power* transcends altogether physical forces, for it controls, guides, directs, arranges, while the latter *are controlled, are guided, are directed,* &c. Power may be said to guide and govern force. Power is one thing and force another.

Some such view as that which I have endeavoured to sketch concerning the nature of life will, I believe, be found to constitute the only possible basis of religious thought regarded from the scientific and philosophical side. Starting from a theory of vitality we may, I apprehend, surely and almost infinitely extend natural religious thought. We may find after all the conflicting arguments shall have been thorougly considered, that reason and faith excite and justify the same hopes and aspirations.

Vitality, it must be remarked, unlike any physical agency yet discovered, manifests a remarkable capacity, so to say, of prevision. The changes effected by *living matter* at one time are carried out as it were in anticipation of future change, as if the conception of what *was to be* had been acted upon even while the early changes were proceeding. Now this preparation for future change is to be noticed from one end of the living world to the other, and with marvellous distinctness as regards the operations of the intellect. For it is unquestionable that in the case of the organ of the mind of man, change paves the way for further change, and each advance renders possible a further onward development, the possibility of which was as it were anticipated almost from the first, though this could never have taken place had not certain preparatory changes, as it were, cleared the way for others which were to result in the formation of the perfect structure.

By the increase or diminution in the number of the bioplasts, the uniformity of the nutritive process as it occurs in all tissues and organs, is preserved. Excess of nutrition is stored up by the increase of bioplasm in times of scarcity.

Vitality cannot be converted into mechanical energy, or other mode of ordinary force, nor can any modes of force be converted into vitality. Vital power is transmitted from living matter to non-living matter *without loss*, and in a manner perfectly peculiar, to which there is nothing analogous in the non-living world.

The particular theory of vitality I have proposed, has met with little favour at the hands of those who have committed themselves to the modern phase of retrograde Epicurean philosophy ; but the principles on which this doctrine of vitality rests, have not been disturbed. The position, indeed, is daily gaining real strength. Not a few opponents very powerful, and armed with weapons they well knew how to wield, have retired from the assault, after having very loudly boasted of what they were about to do. Some have preached and some have prophesied, while others have affirmed, that mighty changes are about to occur, and that extraordinary revolutions in thought were being effected under their auspices. Some have made the strongest assertions concerning the facts and laws they say they *know*, and have exactly defined the precise direction in which the thought of the day is tending, and indicated the line which is to guide its tendency in the time that is to come. An expositor of the physical theory of life has triumphantly declared that many things may be going on beyond the limits of the knowable, and has drawn attention to the intense love of truth manifested by the supporters of the physical doctrine of life, and their hatred of that which, according to the physical dictum, is not true. Opponents of the vital theory have indulged in exclamations about their own beliefs and individual convictions, and in eloquent rhapsodies about what might be seen if it were possible to see under circumstances which unfortunately not only preclude vision, but render existence impossible. After abandoning the safe ground of observation and experiment upon which they used to take their stand, ardent supporters of the physical view appeal to the discoveries of the imagination, to conjecture, and fancy, while their teachings, gradually losing all potentiality, will, it is probable, ere long pass into a latent state, and eventually resume the form of primeval mist and fiery cloud.

For some time past retrograde and long-discarded ancient fancies have been revived and advanced in support of doctrines as hopeless as the materialism of Lucretius. Conjectures recently distilled from the laboratory of the imagination have been forced upon public attention, and though almost identical with some views exploded centuries ago, being habilitated in modern garb escape recognition, and appear to many as new discoveries. Those who do not receive them are called " narrow," " prejudiced," " orthodox," and no wonder that in these days when the consequences of such epithets, especially when hurled with the force pure physicists can alone give, are so disastrous to individuals, the advocates of the truly

G

broad physical dogmas should be very numerous and powerful.*

After having studied the phenomena of living matter for a length of time, and with all the advantages I could obtain, the conviction has been forced upon my mind that vital phenomena must be referred to the influence of an agency distinct from the physical forces of nature. The hypothesis I have been led to adopt is this. I suppose that there is operating upon every particle of every kind of living matter a *forming, guiding, directing power or agency* which is constantly at work, being transmitted from atom to atom. This overcomes, and in a moment, all the ordinary attractions, affinities, and other properties of material molecules and in a manner with which there is nothing comparable in the non-living world. The difference between the lowest simplest germ of living matter and the highest is

* Nevertheless, the amazing confidence displayed by the disciples of the new philosophy, when teaching their views to the unlearned, is very remarkable. All science is now *physics*. Nothing that cannot be comprised under the term *physical* is either scientific or worthy of any thought or consideration. As for the teachings of religion, history, art, and what used to be called philosophy, they are not only absurd but unworthy of refutation. All that these deserve is to be simply ignored, as if they were not and never had been. The physical view, it is arrogantly asserted, is the "scientific view," the physical tendency of thought is the scientific tendency, and so on. All other views and tendencies are not scientific, but frivolous and ridiculous, and only to be *tolerated* for a time by physicists, out of respect for the too slowly waning prejudices due to defective education and the weakness of the public intellect.

not to be accounted for by any difference in composition, but only by supposing a difference in power, which power has been derived and transmitted onwards, as it were, and without loss, from matter having the same power.

Life is not a *consequence* of the organization of matter, but the cause. Life precedes, instead of succeeding organization, conversion, formation. The first impulse is exerted from within the living matter upon the lifeless matter which is brought under the control of vital power. The tendency is from within and is not excited by actions going on around. Living matter always *tends* to grow, move, &c., and when the restrictions under which it is placed are removed, the vital phenomena are manifested with such increased activity as to be readily observable. In the present day writers on the physical side are never tired of urging us to believe that all those marvellous phenomena peculiar to the living world are not peculiar to it at all. Even Mr. Herbert Spencer does not hesitate to assert that " organisms are *highly differentiated* portions of the matter forming the earth's crust and its gaseous envelope." Then he goes on to say, " The chasm between the inorganic and the organic is being filled up." But if this sort of statement is accepted as proof philosophical we may surely prove anything we like and then assert that it has been proved philosophically. He says further that there are organisms the matter of whose bodies is " distinguishable from a

fragment of albumen *only by its finely granular cha-*
racter." * The reader will observe that no facts whatever are adduced in support of these most cleverly
stated assertions.   They do not result from observation or experiment, but rest upon *authority* only.
The " highly differentiated " is not more definite than
Mr. Huxley's "variously modified."   Neither does
the author tell us by what the chasm between the
organic and inorganic is being filled up.   But he is
wise in using the words *organic* and *inorganic* instead
of *living* and *non-living ;* for if these last were substituted for the former the assertion would not be accepted by anyone.   But are not the " distinguishable,"
the " fragment of albumen," and the " finely granular,"
as employed in the above sentence, remarkable for
that vagueness and ambiguity which characterise the
recent developments of material speculations ?

Physiology has been positively affirmed by Herbert
Spencer to be " an interpretation of the physical processes that go on in organisms, in terms known to
physical science," but, seeing how very little physiology can be explained by physical science, and that
of the essential changes which distinguish all living
from all lifeless things, not one can be explained
without " a psychical factor—a factor which no physical research whatever can disclose, or identify, or
get the remotest glimpse of,"—it is clear that such an
interpretation of the " physical processes " as that

* Herbert Spencer, p. 137, vol. i.   Second edition.

indicated will teach us nothing whatever concerning the physiological changes which distinguish all living matter from all non-living matter.

No interpretation of physical processes helps us in the least degree to explain the phenomena which occur in the smallest particle of the simplest form of *living matter* which are due to some agency which acts in a direction *from centre to circumference.* No physical explanation, it need scarcely be remarked, will account for portions of a mass of semi-fluid matter moving away from one another, and in many different directions. In short, no physical explanation will enable us to account for the phenomena of *growth, nutrition, multiplication, formation, conversion,* or other *vital* phenomenon.

Do not the words " physiology," " biology," " pathology," " health," and " disease," imply processes that are not simply physical,—imply in fact a psychical factor? In spite of all that has been urged to the contrary, there is not one of the actions properly called physiological, biological, pathological, healthy, or diseased, that can be regarded as wholly physical, mechanical, or chemical in its nature.

Not only so, but the very terms employed by the physicists themselves in describing phenomena occurring in living beings, and stated by them to be physical, actually imply properties or forces which are not physical. The possession of advantages by certain fortunate creatures in the struggle for existence, is often spoken of as if it depended upon material changes only, but the capability for *enjoying* or profiting by advantages implies something other than physical forces and properties. Living things have been said to resemble crystals in growth and in some other points. But fancy a crystal or other inanimate object *enjoying advantages, or struggling for existence*, or the various forms of carbon or calcareous spar being produced by " natural selection ! " It will be found by any one who takes the trouble to institute the examination, that those who maintain the physical doctrine of life imply by the very language they use the occurrence of non-physical changes which they deny, while they are constantly, but apparently unconsciously, calling in the aid of non-physical factors, " subtle influences," " tendencies," " capacities," " plasticity," and the like, to account for phenomena which they pertinaciously insist are physical.

It comes indeed to this, that unless we ignore the facts of observation, or decline to make any attempts whatever to account for the phenomena of living beings, we must abandon physical explanations which have ever proved incompetent, and resort to hypotheses of another kind. We are really obliged to assume in the case of any form of living matter the existence of a power acting in a direction from within outwards, and the facts necessitate the conclusion that new vital power originates within the very centre of a minute particle of the matter which is alive,—

which is in the peculiar vital state. There is no action
known to occur in non-living matter of any kind
which can in any way be compared with this. Of the
nature of this vital power I can only form some dim
conception from the results of its action, but when
the necessity for the hypothesis of vital power shall
have been admitted, it is likely that rapid advance
will follow in our views concerning the influence
exerted by certain non-physical influences and agencies
in things living, which are now entirely ignored by
physicists.

Thoughtful persons have long felt extremely dis-
satisfied with the material doctrines of life now so
prevalent, and though doubtful concerning the precise
terms in which the influence of some non-physical
power ought to be stated, have acknowledged that the
facts rendered imperative the admission of an agency
belonging to an order very different from that in which
physical and chemical actions are comprised. Such
agencies will be advantageously considered now that
the depressing influence of the physical force tyranny
is happily once more ceasing to retard progress and
oppress thought.

*Of the Action of the Bioplasm concerned in Mental
Action.*—The action of this the highest form which
bioplasm is known to assume, has been carelessly
attributed to physical and chemical change. But
there is not a shadow of fact to justify the dogma
that mind is a form of force. The little bioplasts

described in page 61, and which are probably directly concerned in every kind of intellectual action, are exactly like the bioplasts which exist in every part of the brain, and indeed elsewhere, at an early period of development. They consist almost entirely of living matter, and retain the general characters they exhibited from the first, while life lasts. They vary in number at different periods of life, and increase under certain conditions, like other forms of bioplasm. They are unquestionably more numerous in some spots of the grey matter than in others. Even in the aged these bodies, representing the highest form living matter is yet known to assume, still retain the characters presented by every form of bioplasm at an early period of development.

Their exalted function and wonderful powers could not possibly be predicated from a knowledge of their microscopical characters or chemical composition, or from a knowledge of the properties of the elementary substances into which they may be resolved; but in this respect they agree with every known form of living matter. These wonderfully endowed masses of bioplasm would be called granular particles, and would be classed with other bodies possessing similar characters and of little significance. We should anticipate that of all kinds of bioplasm known, that concerned in mental nervous action would be most evanescent, and prone to rapid change and disintegration after death. It is therefore not surprising that in many cases no traces of the delicate bioplasts I have described should be discovered. I feel sure that what I have been able to demonstrate affords but a very imperfect idea of the very great number and perfect order of the masses, as they exist in the living state. Considering the nature of this form of bioplasm, we should anticipate that change would almost immediately follow the death of the individual, and that these delicate bioplasts would be completely broken down long before other kinds existing in the same organism had ceased to manifest their vital phenomena.

Observation convinces us that the activities manifested by different forms of living matter are dependent, not upon peculiarities of structure or composition, (for these exalted bioplasts look like many forms of mucus and pus corpuscles, and move like small amœbæ and the simplest forms of living matter known), but upon something quite distinct from these, and of a different order altogether. The matter which manifests vital actions possesses no structure, and it is impossible to ascertain its chemical composition, and the objection that structure *might* be discovered, and chemical composition determined if our means of investigation were more perfect than they are, cannot be sustained, and ought never to have been advanced ; for, first, the structure of very many *textures* formed by living beings, and the chemical composition of the same and multitudes of other substances, have been

actually ascertained and demonstrated by means now
at our disposal. If, therefore, the living matter possessed structure, we ought to be able to demonstrate
it. But, secondly, the possession of structural character, and the exhibition of chemical properties, are
actually inconceivable in the case of any form of
matter manifesting vital properties, and, therefore, no
one who was acquainted with the phenomena of
living matter would have suggested that it was likely
to possess structure or consist of matter in the state
of a definite chemical compound.

Since it is at this time impossible to give a sufficient
explanation of the *vital* phenomena of the lowest
simplest forms of living matter in existence (amœba,
monera, &c.), it is not surprising that those marvellous
changes occurring in the most exalted form of living
matter in man's organism should remain unexplained.
That the brain should be represented as a mechanico-
chemical apparatus in which immaterial thought is
elaborated in somewhat the same manner as a
material secretion is secreted by a gland, is, however,
not surprising when we take into consideration the
monstrous assertions which have been made and
credited. Unproven and unprovable statements, such
as the dictum that living things are formed by force—
mind is correlated force—a mode of ordinary
energy—would scarcely be worthy of notice, were it
not that many dicta of the kind have been widely
accepted without due consideration, and without the

suspicion that their acceptance implies and involves very much that the accepter is aware of at the time he assents. Nay, in many cases the physical views are received because it is supposed they are " in advance" of other views. But this is a serious mistake. The recent attempts to interpret vital phenomena by physics are terribly retrograde. Such an interpretation cannot be accepted unless well established truths which cannot be overthrown are purposely ignored, and old ideas, long since proved to be false, are received as true. The advocates of the physical doctrine of life think to force us to revert to views entertained two thousand years ago, and to submit to be guided by an extinct and debasing Epicurean philosophy. This appears to be the aim, and it certainly is the tendency of the popular force philosophy of the present day.

On the other hand, the doctrine of vitality points in an opposite direction. The mind which contemplates vital power will naturally be led to ponder upon the spiritual. The aspirations of the mind will progressively advance, while the intellect increases in strength, encouraged by the hope that it may succeed in forming some conception of the manner in which ever-present, ever-active power designs, guides, and causes to be carried out the never-ceasing changes in living matter.

On the relation of the Non-Living and Living to God.—The general conclusion which it is believed is established by the arguments grounded on facts of observation and experiment advanced in this work is this: that between the *living* and the *non-living* there is an essential—an absolute difference. So far from being unreasonable, it would be in accordance with reason to hold that the relation of ordinary non-living matter to its Creator was not of the same order or nature as that which subsists between God and the power that influences matter in the living state. If this be so, it is also reasonable to conceive that the highest form of vital power of which we have knowledge and experience is in some way yet more closely related to Deity than the vital power which animates the lower forms of bioplasm or living matter. Undoubtedly all such considerations must be accounted null and void as soon as the phenomena manifested by every kind of living matter shall have been fully explained by ordinary forces and by the properties of the material particles of non-living matter ! But since at this time the aid of the hypothesis of vitality, or some other such hypothesis, is required to account for the facts of life, not only is it justifiable to extend our speculations in the direction indicated, but it is for many reasons most desirable that we should do so.

We are led to suppose by the facts known to us that the properties belonging to the different kinds of non-living matter were communicated to it at its origin, and that each elementary molecule of non-living matter has since retained and will ever retain its special characteristic endowments. On the other hand it is conceivable, nay, the conclusion is almost forced upon us, that the peculiar *vital properties or powers* with which living matter is endowed were not acquired until after, perhaps not until very long after, the creation of the matter itself. There is indeed distinct evidence of the existence of vital power of many different kinds, and of change in power acquired during the transmission of vitality from particle to particle, as well as of alteration in the proportion of matter animated during any given time.

It is certain that the inorganic properties and forces have remained the same from the first beginning, and can never be added to or reduced, while it is equally certain that vitality has varied remarkably in quality and distribution at different periods. It is possible for us to conceive an entire cessation of vitality —complete extinction of life after its introduction ; but we cannot conceive of the extinction of matter and its forces after they have once been created. No true analogy can be shown to subsist between the different properties and forces of non-living matter and the different vital powers manifested by the various kinds of living matter. The difference between copper and silver is a difference which exhibits no analogy whatever, and is not comparable with, being in its nature distinct from, the differential characters that distinguish, for instance, the cabbage from the oak. But the very matter that was once cabbage might become at a future

period of time oak. But it is, at least at this time, inconceivable that even in the most distant future, and
under any conceivable alteration of conditions, copper
should become silver, or tin assume the characters of
lead. In the one case there are indeed differences of
form, structure, character, numerous and remarkable
enough, without differences in substance, which will
account for the fact ; in the other there is difference
in substance in the very matter itself.

If all life upon the earth were to cease, the properties and forces of the material particles would still
be retained. In that case the relations and combinations of the elements would be altered, but any trans-
mutation in the matter itself would not occur. Nor
is there reason to think that the relation of our planet
to other worlds would be in the slightest degree disturbed by such a catastrophe.

The reader will naturally inquire if, granting that
all existing life were completely destroyed, we are in
possession of facts which would justify the conclusion that life would at some future time recommence.
It may be answered so far from this being the case we
have ample evidence to lead us to adopt the very
opposite conclusion—that life would never reappear
unless some power able to overcome ordinary tendencies and capable of setting at nought natural laws
intervened. The idea of life is, then, distinct from the
idea of force, property, or matter. *Living* and *formed*
are two distinct qualities of matter which cannot co-

exist in the same particles at the same time. Bioplasm may acquire the properties of *formed* matter, but to do so it must die—it must *lose* its vitality. We have to notice three states of matter as regards living beings—

1. The formless non-living state ; 2. The *living* state ; and, 3. The formed state, in which the matter has acquired certain new characters and endowments, and perhaps exhibits some peculiar *form* which was impressed upon it by vitality. The form and structure of the matter in this formed state may be accepted as *proof* that the very matter was once a part of a being that lived—that it once lived, and that its properties and form resulted directly from the action of vital power.

Vitality is as distinct from matter and material properties as is ever-active mind from the inanimate passive substance which it fashions, and upon which it may impress its own fleeting, and perhaps but momentary conceptions. The many efforts made to prove that vitality is but a mode of force have been as futile as the attempts to show that mind is a property, or a consequence of the changes in, the atoms, whose movements are but the results of its influence and a proof of its presence.

If those who try to make us believe that vitality is derived from the ordinary properties of matter were consistent, they would endeavour to instil the doctrine that the maker of a machine was a consequence of the properties of the materials employed in its construction, and that by its action its constructor was evolved.

Lastly, it may be remarked that the facts hitherto discovered by physiological observation and experiment do not in any way conflict with religious thought. At this very time there would indeed be no inconsistency in holding that a most devout believer and eminent theologian might be at the same time an advanced student in physiological knowledge.

Many statements recently urged with consummate dogmatism by physicists who use very decided language, but have had no experience whatever in other than physical investigation, are undoubtedly incompatible with the acceptance of any religious beliefs, but it has been shown that many of these statements are unworthy of credit, and cannot be proved to rest upon any foundation in fact. After having gained an artificial and forced notoriety they will be discarded as worthless except by the few who have determined to entertain particular scientific views irrespective of evidence.

A theory of vitality (non-material, psychical) will alone enable anyone to account for the facts demonstrated in connection with the life of all living things. Although an immaterial agency cannot be.demonstrated to the senses, the evidences of the working of such a power are so distinct and clear to the reason that the mind which remains unfettered by the tram-

mels of dogmatic physics, and is free to exercise judgment, will not deny its existence.

Although the mental vital action is the highest
manifestation of vital power of which we have any
cognizance, it is not perhaps by any means the highest
manifestation of which the human mind is able to
conceive. As all vital power affects the molecules of
matter, and makes them take up certain positions,
and so arranges them that certain definite combinations shall take place, we may surely conceive the
existence of a vital power capable of causing the
particles it guides to be so arranged as to form at
length complex, and it may be very elaborate structures, performing the most delicate work, and in a
most perfect manner. Such arguments, it seems to
me, further justify a belief in the operation of a
higher agency whose power transcends that of mind
in as great a degree as this last transcends ordinary
vitality. It is by following out such a line of thought
that we may, I think, hope to obtain, even from this
lower physiological stand-point, some dim conception,
it may be, of the nature of Deity, and some idea of
the relation of Deity to man's soul and body, to the
various grades of lower life, and to matter in the
non-living state.

Harri on and Sons, Printers in Ordinary to Her Maje ty, St Martin's Lane

www.ingramcontent.com/pod-product-compliance
Lightning Source LLC
Chambersburg PA
CBHW022338020726
47500CB00004B/1185